D0065896

Don't Open That Box!

I took the box to my room and slammed the door behind me. Then I got out my set of miniature screwdrivers.

I turned the box around to examine the hinges. They were held on by tiny screws. Using the smallest of the screwdrivers, I tried to loosen them.

As I was working, the box seemed to get warmer, which was truly weird. I thought about stopping, but I was dying to see what was inside. After a lot of fussing, I managed to get the screws out. Then I pried the hinges off.

The darn box *still* wouldn't open.

Again, I thought about stopping.

It was too late. Something like fog came pouring over the edge of the box, and a green glow showed through the opening. Suddenly a crackle of tingling energy shot up my fingers. . . .

THE
MONSTERS
OF
MORLEY MANOR

THE MONSTERS OF MORLEY MANOR

Bruce Coville

Magic Carpet Books
Harcourt, Inc.

Orlando   Austin   New York   San Diego   Toronto   London

A significantly different version of *The Monsters of Morley Manor*
was originally serialized in 1996. The author has extensively revised and
expanded the work for this first publication as a complete novel.

www.HarcourtBooks.com

First Magic Carpet Books edition 2003
Magic Carpet Books is a trademark of Harcourt, Inc.,
registered in the United States of America and/or other jursidictions

The Library of Congress has cataloged the hardcover edition as follows:
Coville, Bruce.
The monsters of Morley Manor/Bruce Coville.
p. cm.
Summary: Anthony and his younger sister discover that the monster figures
he got in an unusual box at an estate sale are alive, but they have no way
of knowing that the "monsters" will lead them on fantastical adventures
to other worlds in an effort to try to save Earth.
[1. Extraterrestrial beings—Fiction. 2. Science fiction.]   I. Title.
PZ7.C8344Ml   2001
[Fic]—dc21   00-12912
ISBN 0-15-216382-4
ISBN 0-15-204705-0 pb

Text set in Dante
Designed by Lydia D'moch

A C E G H F D B
Printed in the United States of America

For Willard E. Lape, Jr.,
also known as "Epal"—
early inspiration, current friend, and
still my favorite mad scientist's assistant

Contents

THE
MONSTERS
OF
MORLEY MANOR

1

Morley Manor

IF SARAH HADN'T put the monkey in the bathtub, we might never have had to help the monsters get big. But she did, so we did, which, given the way things worked out, was probably just as well for everyone on the planet—especially the dead people.

I bought the monsters at a garage sale. Actually, it was more like a whole house sale. And not just any house. It was Morley Manor, the huge old place at the end of Willow Street.

Every kid in our town knew Morley Manor. It

was the weirdest house in Owl's Roost, Nebraska, so scary we didn't even trick-or-treat there. It had three towers, leaded glass windows, and a big iron fence with spikes on the top—though you couldn't see that much of the fence, because the base was overgrown with enormous weeds. Each tower had a lightning rod, which is probably the only reason the place hadn't burned down. Lightning seemed to strike there a lot. My father used to claim that Morley Manor had its own weather system; not only was it darker and gloomier than anywhere else in town, it seemed to be the focus of every thunderstorm that passed through.

I was in sixth grade the year Old Man Morley died. (I know it's not very polite to call him that, but it was the name everyone in town, including the old people, used.) He didn't leave a will, and as far as anyone knew he didn't have any relatives. So the state claimed the house and put it up for sale. Despite the fact that we all thought the place was weird, we were really upset to find out that the guy who finally bought it planned to tear the old mansion down and build a new house altogether.

"You can't blame him," said my mother, when we were discussing this in the back room of the flower shop that she and Dad own. "I can't imagine anyone wanting to live in that old monstrosity."

She adjusted a chrysanthemum, looked at it critically, then pulled it out of the vase and threw it away.

What she said about Morley Manor was true enough, I suppose. But I knew I was going to miss the house, since it was the most interesting place in town.

Of course, being the most interesting place in Owl's Roost, Nebraska, isn't all that hard.

Anyway, the weekend before the wreckers were supposed to start, my parents went to a florists convention in Los Angeles, leaving Gramma Walker to take care of me and my little sister, Sarah. Gramma had been staying with us a lot since Grampa died three months earlier, so Sarah and I were used to having her around. Gramma's pretty deaf, which can make it hard to talk to her. But we never minded when Mom and Dad left her to take care of us. Why would we, when she tended to bake cookies on a daily basis and was a lot less strict about us eating in the living room?

That same weekend the new owner of Morley Manor had a sale to get rid of all the junk inside. Sarah and I figured he was going to use the money to pay the wreckers.

The sale was on a Sunday afternoon. The demolition was supposed to start the next morning, which was Columbus Day. Since we kids had the day off from school, most of us were planning to be there to watch.

Just about everyone in town went to the sale, even though it was pouring rain. After all, it was the only chance we'd ever have to get a look inside the old place. We asked Gramma if she wanted to come with us, but she said no. She acted kind of weird about it, too. But then, she had been a little odd ever since Grampa died. I could understand. His funeral was the worst day of my life, and I knew Gramma loved him even more than I did, though that was hard to imagine. I hadn't slept very well for the first month after he died, and I had cried a lot. I still have one of his old pipes in my sock drawer. Sometimes I take it out and smell it, just to remember him better.

Anyway, with Mom and Dad out of town, and Gramma Walker deciding to "be a homebody," Sarah and I went to the sale on our own, sheltering ourselves from the pelting rain with the big black umbrella that used to belong to Grampa.

"You sure you don't want to go?" we asked again, just before we left.

Gramma shook her head. "It makes me too sad."

"Why does it make you sad?" asked Sarah. Asking questions is sort of a hobby with her. She's like a hunter-gatherer for information. When she was a baby, and I swear I'm not making this up, her first word wasn't "mommy" or "daddy" or even "no." It was "why."

She's been saying it about three thousand times a day ever since.

Gramma sighed. "I'd just rather remember the house the way it used to be."

"You've been *inside* Morley Manor?" I asked in astonishment. As far as we kids knew, no one except Mr. Morley had been inside the place for years.

"Oh, I used to go visit there all the time," she said. "Until—"

Her face got all puckered up, and she shook her head. "Oh, it's not something I like to talk about," she said. "Now you children run along and have a good time."

Then she shooed us out the door.

Sarah and I stood on the porch for a minute, just looking at each other.

"Do you suppose she knows what it was?" she asked at last.

By "it" she meant the horrible thing that had happened at Morley Manor fifty years ago. Every kid in town knew that something had happened there. But none of us knew what it was.

"Could be," I said. "We're going to have to work on her."

That would be mostly Sarah's job, of course. As

the family's official question machine, she could be counted on to do everything possible to dig out the information.

"OOOH, THIS PLACE *is* spooky," said Sarah as we walked through the big iron gate at the entrance to Morley Manor. "*Really* spooky," she added, after we had climbed the porch and stepped inside.

I thought about shouting "boo!" just to see if I could get her to jump, but decided against it. There were too many people around.

Besides, something about Morley Manor made you feel like you ought to be quiet. It had high ceilings, dark woodwork, and doors just as creaky as you would have expected. You could see it must have been beautiful once, but you could also see why no one wanted to live in it now. It looked as if that weather system my father talked about had existed inside as well as outside. The house was damp and moldy, and peeling wallpaper hung down in long strips, leaving bare spots where dark patches of mildew had started to grow. But it wasn't just the look of the place that made it spooky; it was the *feeling* you got when you were inside. I can't really explain it, since I had never felt anything like it. Let's just say that it was easy to imagine secret passages with weird things lurking in them—things waiting to get you if you were stupid enough to be in there after dark.

I found a lot of stuff I wanted to buy: weird little statues, candleholders shaped like demons, a chess set with stone pieces that looked like they had been carved out of someone's nightmare. But they were all too expensive; *way* too expensive, given the fact that I had spent almost all my money on a new batch of trading cards a few days earlier.

Then Sarah found something I thought maybe I *could* afford, though it was hard to tell, since it didn't have a price tag. Herbie Fluke, one of the kids from my class, and I were studying a roped-off stairway that had a sign saying ABSOLUTELY NO ONE PAST THIS POINT and discussing what would happen if we *did* go past that point, when Sarah grabbed my sleeve and said, "Come here, Anthony. I want to show you something!"

I didn't go right away; I didn't want Herbie getting the idea I'll do something just because my kid sister wants me to. But after a minute I followed her to the library. (Yeah, Morley Manor was so fancy it had its own library. Only, the place smelled pretty bad, because the books had gotten all moldy, which I thought was really sad.)

"Look!" she said proudly.

Sitting on a small round table was something that

looked like a wooden cigar box. Carved into its top was a strange design of interlocking circles.

"I didn't see that when I was in here before," I said.

"It was hidden behind the encyclopedia," replied Sarah, nodding toward one of the shelves. "This old guy was looking through stuff in here, and he pointed it out to me. I thought you might want it for your cards."

I snorted. "I couldn't fit all my cards in there!"

"I know *that*. But when you go to shows and swaps and stuff, it would be good for carrying the best ones."

She was right, but I didn't want to admit it too quickly. I lifted the box and gave it a good looking-over, checking to make sure it was solid and didn't have any rot or anything. Then I sniffed it, because I didn't want to take home something that smelled all mildewy. To my surprise, it had a kind of spicy odor.

"It's locked," I said, wrinkling my brow.

"So? You can take care of that."

Sometimes I get the impression Sarah thinks I can do anything—which is nice, but also a little nerve-racking, since I don't want to do anything that would show I can't. In this case she was probably right; I could find some way to open the box. I flipped it over again to see how much it cost.

"It doesn't have a price tag," I said disapprovingly.

Sarah rolled her eyes. "So go *ask* how much they want for it. It probably won't be that much. And remember, you don't have to pay what they ask for the first time. People *always* make deals at this kind of sale."

"I know that!" I said. (Which was true, if you considered that I knew it now that she had said it. I figured she was probably right, since she had been to enough garage sales with my mother to be an expert by now.)

I looked at the box for a minute longer. Then, mostly to put off making a decision, I suggested we go look at some other stuff. I hid the box under the desk before we left the room so no one would buy it while I was making up my mind.

Going off to look at other stuff was fine with Sarah; she loves this kind of old junk. But I couldn't stop thinking about the box, and after a few minutes I went back to examine it again.

Finally I took it to the gray-haired woman sitting at the card table in the front room. I didn't recognize her, and wondered if the new owner had brought in someone from out of town to run the sale, to make sure he didn't get cheated. Or maybe she *was* the new owner.

"So . . . how much do you want for this dumb box?" I asked, trying to sound cool.

She took it from my hands, studied it for a moment, then said, "Five dollars."

I could feel my eyes bulge, but I tried not to make a choking sound. "How about a dollar?" I asked.

The woman laughed out loud. I could feel myself start to blush.

"Two dollars?" I asked.

"Four," she replied, without batting an eye.

Well, that was progress. Maybe Sarah was right.

"How about two-fifty?" I suggested. As I did, I realized something weird: Now that I had started to try to buy the box, I *really* wanted it, so much that it was almost scary.

The woman narrowed her eyes. "Three-fifty," she said in a firm voice.

And that was as low as she would go. Which was a lot better than five, but still a problem, since I only had two dollars and thirty-seven cents in my pocket. (When I realized *that,* I was actually relieved that she hadn't said yes to my offer of two-fifty, since I would have looked really stupid counting out the change and coming up thirteen cents short.)

I thought about going home and trying to hit up my grandmother for some money. But I was afraid someone would buy the box while I was gone, even if I hid it again.

So I went to see if I could squeeze some money out of Sarah.

I found her in one of the bedrooms, trying on old hats.

"Do you like this?" she asked when I came into the room. She was wearing something blue and fuzzy that didn't look bad on her.

"It looks stupid," I said, just like I always did when she asked if I liked something.

She made a face. "Don't be such a snot, Anthony."

She was right. I shouldn't be a snot, especially if I wanted to borrow money from her. She noticed I was carrying the box. "Did you buy it?" she asked, looking pleased.

I shook my head. "I don't have enough money. How much do you have?"

She looked nervous.

"I'll pay you back," I said, exasperated.

"You still owe me a dollar from last week."

"I've got it at home. You just never asked for it."

"I did, too!"

"Look, all I need is a dollar and thirteen cents."

She frowned. "I want to buy this hat."

The hat was a dollar-fifty. Sarah had two dollars. I felt as if I was trapped in a math problem.

"Let's see if we can make a deal," said Sarah.

The woman didn't look exactly pleased to see me, so I let Sarah do the talking. Having a cute little sister is not always a bad thing. Sarah twinkled and pleaded and pouted, and next thing I knew, the woman had sold us both the hat and the box for four dollars and thirty cents.

We argued all the way home about how much I owed Sarah.

The argument stopped when we walked through the front door and Mr. Perkins bit me.

2

Monkey Business

MR. PERKINS is my mother's monkey. Mom bought him last year when she turned forty. She said she had always wanted a monkey when she was a kid, but her parents wouldn't let her have one.

"I can have a midlife crisis or a midlife monkey," she announced on her fortieth birthday. "I've decided to go for the monkey."

My father wasn't entirely amused, but he decided having a monkey was better than having my mother go bananas. (I think he was secretly afraid that if we didn't get the monkey she might decide she wanted to have another baby instead.)

Anyway, that's how we got Mr. Perkins.

I have to admit that up until the day we actually got the little beast I had figured it would be cool to have a monkey. Then Mom brought him home, and I found out how loud, smelly, and cranky monkeys really are.

Also that they like to pee on your head, which Mr. Perkins has done twice to me.

Anyway, when we came through the door, Mr. Perkins was lurking on top of the coat tree, which is one of his favorite places. As soon as he saw us, he jumped down and bit me on the ankle. Not hard enough to break the skin; I swear he knows that if he did that Mom would get rid of him. No, he just bit hard enough to startle me into yelling and dropping the box.

Instantly, Mr. Perkins grabbed it and ran away, as if he knew that was the thing he could do that would bother me most.

"Hey!" I shouted. "You bring that back!"

Sarah and I began chasing the monkey around the house, making so much noise that after a while even Gramma Walker heard the uproar and came to help us.

(Gramma Walker is my father's mother, by the

way. My mother's mother won't visit us now that Mom has a monkey. She takes it personally.)

Working together, the three of us finally cornered Mr. Perkins behind my father's reading chair, and I managed to get the box back.

"Man, I hope he didn't scratch it," I said bitterly, examining the wood for any sign of damage. But the box was not harmed, which relieved me more than I would have expected.

The only good thing about all the fuss was that by the time it was over Sarah gave up bugging me about how much money I owed her—probably because she could tell I was in such a totally bad mood it wouldn't do her any good.

I took the box into my room and slammed the door behind me. Then I got out my set of miniature screwdrivers. Grampa Walker had given them to me for my last birthday, which had been just a month before he died. He gave them to me because I had always liked to play with them when I visited him at the farm. He used to use them for the model railroads he liked to build, but he had dropped that hobby when his hands got too shaky.

Sometimes I wondered if the reason he had passed them on to me was that he knew he was going to die soon.

After carefully unwrapping the screwdrivers,

which Grampa had kept folded in a black cloth pouch, I began to study the box. How was I supposed to open the thing? I tried sticking the smallest screwdriver into the keyhole and wiggling it around. No luck. I didn't want to break the lock, though I was willing to do that if I had to. But I wasn't sure I could do it without damaging the wood, and that I did not want to do.

I turned the box around to examine the hinges. They were held on by tiny screws. Still using the smallest of the screwdrivers, I tried to loosen them.

As I was working, the box seemed to get warmer, which was truly weird. I thought about stopping, but my curiosity had the best of me, and I was dying to see what was inside. After a lot of fussing, I managed to get the screws out. Then I pried the hinges off.

The darn box *still* wouldn't open.

Frustrated, I poked the tip of a slightly larger screwdriver between the lid and the body of the box and tried to ease them apart. Just when I was about to stop, for fear of breaking Grampa's screwdriver, the lid made a horrible squeak and moved up about a half an inch. At the same time my desk lamp began to flicker.

Again, I thought about stopping.

It was too late. Something like fog came pouring over the edge of the box, and a green glow showed through the opening. Suddenly a crackle of tingling energy shot up my fingers.

"Yow!" I cried.

When I let go of the lid it slammed back onto the body of the box so fast it was almost as if it had been sucked down.

I stared at the box, torn between terror and a deep curiosity. When I finally got up enough courage, I reached forward and touched it again, just a little tap with the tip of my finger.

I pulled my hand back quickly.

Nothing happened.

I tried again.

Still nothing.

Must have been some weird buildup of static electricity, I told myself. But I wasn't entirely convinced. I decided to go get something to eat, mostly as a way of putting off making a decision about opening the box. Part of me had begun to think it was a bad idea. Part of me was dying to see what was inside. (And yet another part of me was afraid that once I did get it open, I would find nothing interesting at all, which was a different kind of scary.)

I had lunch, then watched some cartoons with Sarah, which is fun, because you can really bug her by telling her how stupid the plots for *Scooby-Doo* always are.

Two hours later I went back into my room. *It's just a box, for pete's sake!* I told myself.

Even so, I was plenty nervous as I slid it toward me to try to open it again.

The lid creaked as I pried it up, but this time there was no fog, no tingle. I did see the green glow again, but it vanished as soon as I got the lid all the way open—sort of the reverse of the light in the refrigerator.

Underneath the lid was . . . another lid! This one was made of wood, too, though a lighter shade, and had a pair of knobs, one on each side, which I figured were for lifting it out. Painted in the center was a fancy circle. In the center of the circle, written in bold black letters, were the words MARTIN MORLEY'S LITTLE MONSTERS.

Below that, in very fine print, it said, OPEN NOT THIS BOX LEST MY CURSE FALL UPON YOU.

"Yeah, right," I muttered. It looked like Old Man Morley was even kookier than everyone had thought.

Grabbing the knobs, I pulled out the second lid. I gasped in delight.

The box was divided into five compartments. And inside each compartment was a metal statue of a tiny monster. Three appeared to be male, two female. They were very detailed, beautifully made, and extremely weird.

At the base of each compartment was an engraved nameplate. I had to rub them clean with a tissue before I could read them.

I blinked. According to the nameplates, the monsters' names were Gaspar, Albert, Ludmilla, Melisande, and Bob.

"Weird names for a bunch of monsters," I muttered as I picked up Gaspar. (At least, I assumed it was Gaspar. It was possible someone had played with the monsters and put them back in the wrong slots.)

The little monster was about five inches tall. He had a head like a lizard's, stuck on top of a muscular, manlike body. A spiny crest rose from the top of his head then disappeared under the neck of his lab coat. A long, powerful tail extended from the back of his ragged trousers. He looked (and felt) as if he were made of solid brass. I fooled around with him a little, making him bounce across my desk and growl and stuff. Then I stood him at the edge of the box, and took out the next figurine, which was Albert.

Albert was about an inch shorter than Gaspar, and seemed to be a typical mad scientist's assistant—a fierce-looking hunchback with shaggy hair and a squinty face. His hands stretched forward in a grabbing gesture, as if he had been frozen in midaction. Whoever had made him was really good. He even had a patch sewed into the back of his coarse tunic to make room for his hump. It was all done in brass, of course. But the effect was very realistic.

Still holding Albert, I looked at the others. Ludmilla was sort of a vampire lady. She had a cape wrapped around her, big eyes, and a pair of fangs that poked down over her lower lip. Melisande had snakes for hair. Bob looked like your basic wolfman—a human form with a snarling, wolflike face that was, oddly enough, kind of cute. He was in a slight crouch, as if ready to spring at something.

The detail work on all five of the monsters was amazing; Melisande's face, for example, had tiny, delicate scales, and she was wearing a slinky, skintight dress that seemed to have scales, also. I began to wonder if the figurines might be more valuable than I had expected.

I was about to set Albert next to Gaspar so I could examine Ludmilla when Sarah shrieked, "Anthony! *Help!*"

Her voice was coming from the bathroom. Still holding Albert, I pushed away from my desk and raced down the hall.

The bathroom door was half open. I could hear running water and angry chattering. I groaned. Sarah was trying to give Mr. Perkins a bath again!

"You get back in that tub!" she ordered the monkey as I came through the door.

The floor was like a swamp. Sarah was half soaked herself, and her damp hair lay flat on her forehead. Mr. Perkins, soaking wet, clung to my sister's neck, screeching and hissing.

What really griped me was that he didn't bite her, and probably wouldn't, no matter how angry he got. Me he bites out of sheer cussedness. My pukey little sister could tie a knot in his tail and he still wouldn't set tooth in her skin.

"Anthony!" cried Sarah again. *"Help!"*

What did she expect me to do? If I got near the monkey he was sure to take a chunk out of me. I set Albert on the back of the toilet and made a couple of moves as if to help Sarah. But my heart wasn't in it, especially when Mr. Perkins turned toward me and bared those nasty little fangs.

I really don't know what my mother was thinking when she bought him.

As it turned out, Sarah didn't really need my help. A minute later, she had Mr. Perkins off her neck and back in the bathtub.

It was like turning on a blender. Water splashed all over the place.

When we were finally done shampooing and toweling Mr. Perkins (I helped with the toweling, because he couldn't bite me through the thick cloth), I noticed that some water had splashed onto Albert's hand. When I said something about it, Sarah wanted to know where the little monster had come from. I ended up showing her the whole set, which she thought was pretty cool.

Two more strange things happened that night. The first came after supper, when we were cleaning up the kitchen. Gramma had been reading the newspaper and had left it on the table. Sarah glanced at it, then grabbed my arm.

"Anthony!" she hissed. *"That's him!"*

"Who's him?" I asked. "What are you talking about?"

"Him," she said, pointing to the paper. "That's the old man who showed me the box you bought today!"

I picked up the paper and felt a cold chill shiver down my spine. The paper was a few days old, and the article was about the sale to be held at Morley Manor—the sale we had gone to that day. And the picture? It was labeled, "Martin Morley, recently deceased owner of Morley Manor."

"You're crazy," I said. "He's dead."

"He may be dead," replied Sarah, "but I swear I saw him."

She looked really nervous.

I didn't believe her. I didn't *want* to believe her.

But I couldn't stop thinking about it.

As if that wasn't enough, something even stranger happened when I was getting ready to go to bed. I hadn't thought any more about Albert's hand getting wet, until I decided to take a last look at the monsters before I went to sleep.

Then I saw that his hand had changed color, the brass tones transformed to a dark, fleshy shade.

I got mad, because I figured the water had damaged whatever Albert was made of. But when I touched his hand I drew my finger back, my anger quickly shifting to fear.

The little monster's hand was no longer hard and metallic. Now it felt warm—warm and . . . fleshy.

I picked up the figurine and stared at it.

To my horror, its fingers began to move.

3

Just Add Water

 I SLAPPED ALBERT back into the box, closed the lid, and latched it. Then I put the box in the bottom drawer of my desk, closed the drawer, and locked that, too.

But I didn't leave it there.

I couldn't.

Which isn't to say I didn't try. But I couldn't sleep, thinking about that tiny hand, stretching and grasping. It was horrifying—but not as horrifying as the idea that a living creature was locked, frozen, in my desk. A creature I could revive just by adding water. If Mr. Perkins hadn't splashed him, if I hadn't seen that hand move, I would never have known, and it wouldn't have made any difference. But I did know, and because I did know it seemed to me that I had to do something about it. The thought of keeping some tiny person frozen (or statued, or whatever) was too awful to live with.

Unfortunately, the idea of bringing him completely to life was pretty awful as well. After all, it was possible he had been frozen for a reason. What kind of monster was he, anyway?

Well, a small one, to begin with. It wasn't as if he could tear me limb from limb or anything.

After fussing like this for an hour or so, I got out of bed, slipped into my robe, and went to my desk.

I took out the box and opened it.

Albert's fist was still moving, clenching and unclenching, a bit of living flesh stuck on a lifeless metallic figurine. I took a deep breath, then whispered, "All right, buddy, let's thaw you out."

I tucked Albert into the pocket of my robe, then stepped into the hall. It was dark and quiet. I hoped Mr. Perkins was asleep and not just hiding somewhere, getting ready to jump on my head and pee on me again.

About halfway down the hall, I stopped and went

back to Sarah's room. I stood outside her door, trying to decide whether to wake her. Part of me wanted to do this on my own, keep it all to myself. Another part of me thought it would be a good idea to have someone else along, just in case things got out of hand—and so I would have someone to talk to about it. Also, it's always better to have Sarah along when I'm doing something that might get me in trouble, since my parents never seem to get as mad when she's involved.

Finally I knocked on her door, then pushed it open and hissed, "Sarah! Wake up!"

She moaned. "What do you want, Anthony?" (She doesn't like waking up, especially in the middle of the night.)

"I have to show you something."

She sat up fast, and I remembered that the last time I woke her and said those words, I had also dropped a snake onto her bed.

"This is different," I said urgently. I turned on the lamp next to her bed as I spoke, then thrust Albert into the cone of light.

Sarah gasped at the sight of his tiny moving fingers. Scooching back against the wall, she whispered, "Anthony, that is *too* weird." She shuddered, then asked, "How did you do it?"

"It happened when he got wet. I'm going to go get the rest of him wet now."

Sarah grabbed my arm. "Do you think you should?"

"I have to. It's not right to leave him like this."

"Maybe he's that way for a reason," said Sarah, who is very big on being sensible. "Maybe he's *evil*."

"Maybe whoever froze him was evil."

Sarah thought about that for a moment. Though she's big on being sensible, she's also big on compassion. She'll probably be a vegetarian in a year or so. "How can we find out?" she whispered at last.

"Unfreeze him."

"What if it turns out that he *is* evil?"

"We'll squash him!"

I said that with more certainty than I actually felt, and I had a brief vision of Albert escaping and hiding in the walls, then sneaking out at night to torment us. But just as I was about to change my mind about thawing him out, Sarah said, "Okay, let's do it!"

She slipped out of bed and grabbed a flashlight from her nightstand. We both used to have flashlights, but I had lost mine.

We tiptoed down the hallway—though we didn't really need to; Gramma Walker is so hard of hearing we probably could have stomped to the bathroom without waking her up.

Albert's tiny hand continued stretching and grasping, something I could see all too well by the glow of Sarah's flashlight.

"What do we do now?" asked Sarah, when we got to the bathroom.

"Get him wet," I replied. I looked at him for a second, then added, "Should we sprinkle him, or dunk him?"

Sarah thought about it. "Dunk him," she said at last. "It would be really gross if he came to life in little spots all over his body. Dangerous, too, maybe. I mean for him."

I wasn't sure what the medical rules were for bringing a monster back to life. But I decided Sarah was right.

So we filled the sink. I dipped Albert into the water, planning to pull him right back out. But as soon as I put him in, the water began bubbling and boiling, splashing over the edge of the sink like some sort of weird chemical reaction. I dropped Albert and jumped back with a yelp. A weird green glow came from the sink.

Sarah huddled against me. I didn't push her away.

When the water calmed down, I saw a little hand thrust through the surface.

"He's drowning!" hissed Sarah. "Go save him, Anthony!"

I started forward, but Albert was already hauling himself onto the edge of the sink. He shook his head, spattering tiny drops of water in all directions. Then he stood, looked around, scratched his head, and said, "Oy, now what has the boss gotten me into?"

He started to walk along the edge of the basin. "What a strange white road," he muttered.

I cleared my throat.

Albert glanced up at me and Sarah. "Yikes!" he screamed. *"Monsters!"*

Then he dived back into the sink.

I hurried over and looked in. Albert was at the bottom of the basin, clinging to the drain plug. I didn't do anything at first, but when I began to be afraid he might drown, I reached in and pulled him out. He pounded on my fingers as I lifted him. I half expected him to bite me in order to get me to drop him, but that was probably only because I've spent so much time with Mr. Perkins.

Albert didn't bite. He just squirmed like a demented squirrel, shouting, "Let me go, you big brute! I never did nothing to you."

"Hey, hey," I said softly, "I'm not going to hurt you. I thawed you out, didn't I?"

He blinked, and a series of expressions raced across his face, shifting through surprise, understanding, anger, fear, and back to understanding. "Uh-oh," he said. "I think we've got a little problem here." Looking up at me, he asked in a suspicious voice, "What are you, anyway?"

"I'm a kid."

His eyes got wider. "How did you get so big?"

"How'd you get so small?" I responded.

We stared at each other for a moment. As far as I was concerned, I wasn't all that big. Heck, if I *was*, I wouldn't have so many problems with Ralph Mangram at school. But I was certainly big compared to Albert. At first I had figured that the little guy had somehow gotten shrunk, but now I wondered if he was from some other world. Maybe he had always been this size, and we humans were giants compared to his people!

"Would you put me down, please?" he asked softly.

I set him on the edge of the sink, then knelt so that we were face-to-face. His head was about the size of my eyeball. Sarah knelt next to me.

"Where are you from?" she asked.

"Brooklyn, originally," said Albert.

"Brooklyn?" I asked.

"Yeah, you know, as in New York City. Then I lived in Transylvania for a while."

Well, those were both on Earth. So much for the other-world theory.

Sounding nervous, Albert asked, "Where am I now?"

"Owl's Roost, Nebraska," said Sarah proudly.

Albert's eyes widened. "But that's where I live!" He swallowed. "You . . . you're not giants, are you?"

Sarah and I shook our heads.

Albert sat down, cross-legged, his shoulders drooping, his hump nearly as high as his head. "I've been shrunk!" he moaned. He sounded really depressed. I suppose you couldn't blame him. Suddenly he jumped to his feet. "Where are the others?"

"In the box," I replied.

"The box?"

"The box you came in," explained Sarah.

"Well, go get them! Then we have to figure out a way to get back to our normal size." He looked around, then said, "Wait a minute. What year is this? It *is* 1948, isn't it?"

From the tone of his voice, I could tell he had a pretty good idea that it *wasn't* 1948. But when I told him he was off by more than fifty years, he screamed.

"Martin did this! Oh, I knew he was up to no good. Come on, we *have* to wake up the others!"

"What's the hurry?" I asked, not sure I wanted to deal with *five* little monsters.

Albert leaped from the sink, grabbed the front of my pajamas, and scrambled up my chest like a sailor climbing a ship's rigging. I jumped backward and tried to brush him off, but he was too strong. Once he had reached my shoulder he stuck his head in my ear and bellowed, "The hurry is, they're my family and I don't want them frozen! Besides, I'm not the smart one. We need Gaspar and Ludmilla. *Now go get them!*"

Jeez. And I thought Mr. Perkins was a problem.

We started down the hall to fetch the other monsters, Albert riding in the big pocket on the left side of my bathrobe. Sarah positioned herself on the other side of me, then tugged my sleeve and whispered, "Anthony, do you think this is a good idea?"

"It's probably a terrible idea," I replied. "But it's the most interesting thing we've ever done. Besides, I don't think we could talk Albert out of it. And even if we could . . ."

Sarah nodded as my voice trailed off. I sensed that, like me, she was thinking about the little monsters having been frozen (or whatever) for over fifty years. It was time to thaw them out.

When we got to my room, I set Albert on my desk. He ran to the box. "Boss!" he cried in horror when he saw Gaspar. "Oh, boss, boss, what has that maniac done to you?"

"I take it he didn't always look like that?" I asked, picking up the lizard-headed monster.

"I'm not worried about how he looks, you idiot," Albert said. "We can change *that*. It's the fact that he's been shrunk and turned into a statue that has me upset." He walked along the front of the box, gazing into each compartment. "Poor Melisande," he sighed. "Poor Ludmilla. Asleep for over half a century."

"Not what you'd call sleeping beauties," I remarked.

"Beauty is as beauty does," snapped Albert. He stopped in front of the last slot, the one with the wolfman-type guy. "Alas, poor Bob," he said, patting the figurine on the head. "Trapped in this horrible form all these years."

"So Bob didn't always look like that, either?" asked Sarah.

Albert shook his head. "Only occasionally. He's were."

"Were what?" I asked. Then I got it. "Oh! You mean he's a werewolf?"

"Not quite," said Albert. "Come on, let's stop with the jabbering and wake them up."

I put Gaspar back in the box, then picked up the whole set. With Albert on my shoulder and Sarah at my side, I headed back to the bathroom.

It was monster time.

4

The Family
Morleskievich

PUTTING ALBERT in the sink had made it act like a bubbling stew pot. Dropping in four monsters at once just about turned it into a geyser. Water sprayed everywhere, coming out so forcefully it hit the ceiling (not to mention splashing all over me and Sarah). As before, a weird green glow lit the water from within.

The bubbling stopped. The glow faded. Four coughing, gagging little monsters climbed out of the sink. They were wet, bedraggled, and extremely confused. But they were also overjoyed to see one another.

"Melisande!" shouted Ludmilla.

"Ludmilla!" shouted Melisande.

They threw their arms around each other and hugged. Then Melisande looked up and spotted me and Sarah. Her snakes began writhing in horror, and she let out a scream.

It was amazingly loud for someone so tiny.

I heard an answering scream, and realized Mr. Perkins was on the prowl. I wondered if he thought Melisande was another monkey. I shut the bathroom door, just to be safe.

The other monsters had looked up when Melisande screamed. Their eyes went wide and they cowered together—except for Gaspar, the lizard-headed guy. He just closed his eyes and heaved a deep sigh.

Despite Albert's attempts to assure Ludmilla and Melisande that Sarah and I were friendly, it took several minutes for them to settle down. When they finally did, Albert introduced first Sarah, then me.

"They were the ones who disenchanted us," he said, sounding at least as surprised as he was grateful.

Gaspar looked up at us, then made a deep bow. It was clear he wasn't used to doing that, because he bumped his nose against the sink. He stood up and straightened his lab coat, obviously trying to pretend the bump had not happened. In a deep voice, with his long tongue flicking in and out, he said, "My profound thanks to you for releasing me and my family from our imprisonment."

Albert had said something about family, too.

"So you guys are all, like, related?" I asked.

Gaspar smiled—which was somewhat terrifying, given how many teeth he had. "Well, Albert isn't actually family—though he has worked for me for so long that it often feels as if he is. But Ludmilla and Melisande are my sisters. And Bob is our faithful dog."

"Dog?" cried Sarah. "I thought he was a werewolf!"

Gaspar made a hissing noise, which I found very disturbing until I finally realized it was laughter.

"Bob is a were*human*," he explained. "Most of the time he's a cocker spaniel. But when the moon is full he turns into something sort of like a human being. It's very frightening for him."

Bob whined in agreement.

Gaspar tapped the end of his own long face and said, "Hmmm. There must be a full moon tonight, or Bob would have returned to his normal form. At least, I think he would. It's hard to say how what we have been through would affect his condition."

"How did you get so small?" Sarah asked.

Gaspar's eyes grew wide. "Treachery!" he replied, raising a clenched fist into the air. "Foul, foul treachery. It was the work of my brother, Martin. He was the one who shrank us."

"Did he turn you into monsters, too?" I asked.

"Oh, no!" hissed Melisande, the words coming from the snakes on her head rather than from her mouth. "We did that ourssselvessss! Only we don't like the word monsssterssss. We prefer to ssssay we are . . . ssspecial."

"You *wanted* to be mons—er . . . special?" asked Sarah in astonishment.

Ludmilla smiled, showing her fangs. "Vell, it seemed like a good idea at the time." Her accent reminded me of Bela Lugosi in *Dracula*. Since none of the others had that accent, and since she was supposed to be their sister, I wondered if she was faking it, or if it came with the transformation that had made her a vampire to begin with.

Bob sat down and tried to scratch behind his left ear with his foot. He couldn't quite manage it, though.

Melisande patted his head sympathetically, then scratched behind the ear for him.

"Do you know where our enemy is?" asked Gaspar, his forked tongue flicking between his thin lips. "Now that we are free, there is a score to settle, and we must—"

Albert tugged at his lab coat. "Listen, boss, there's something you need to know."

"What?" asked Gaspar impatiently.

"We've been sleeping for over fifty years!"

Gaspar threw back his head and hissed in rage. He clenched his fists and waved them at the ceiling. His thick tail thrashed back and forth. "Perfidy upon perfidy!" he cried. "Now does the world say, 'Gaspar, you were a fool, a fool to trust your scheming brother.'" He staggered, then gasped. "Ethel! What about Ethel?"

"Now, boss," said Albert. "Don't get yourself in a state."

"Who's Ethel?" asked Sarah.

Gaspar dropped his hands to his sides. Chest heaving, he said, "I don't wish to speak of it." He narrowed his eyes. "Does Martin still live?"

I hesitated, not sure how he would take the news.

"Well?" he demanded.

"Well," I said, "if Martin was the guy we used to call Old Man Morley, he died last month."

Gaspar hissed again. "No chance to say good-bye. No time to heal old wounds. O world, o world, why must you be so dark?" Suddenly he stood up straight and declared, "We have to get back to the house as soon as possible!"

"Why?" asked Sarah.

"It issss the only way for ussss to return to our proper ssssizzzze," hissed the snakes on Melisande's head, writhing in agitation.

"The only way?" I asked nervously.

"Absolutely," said Gaspar. He sounded desperate. "Everything we need is in my laboratory—not only the scientific equipment but also the ingredients for my spells."

"You use science *and* magic?" asked Sarah.

"Vy does that surprise you?" asked Ludmilla, showing her fangs.

Sarah shrugged "I don't know. It just seems weird."

"Sarah's right," I said, which were words I almost never spoke. "In the movies they always use either science *or* magic to do stuff, but not both."

Gaspar sighed, as if it was an old argument. "That represents a small-minded view of the world," he said. "But then, people always do like to put things in little boxes."

I didn't mention that *he* had been in a little box when I found him.

"It's like thinking that an artist should either paint pictures or make statues, but not both," he continued. "But what law says you can't combine things? After all, the ancient Greeks used to paint their statues."

I looked at him in surprise. "Are you positive about that? I've seen pictures of those statues. They sure didn't look painted to me."

"It wore off," snapped Gaspar. His tongue flicked

over his sharp little teeth, giving him a dangerous look.

I decided not to argue.

"The point is," he said, a little more calmly, "you should not limit your possibilities."

"Actually, boss," put in Albert, "the main point right now is that we have to get back to Morley Manor if we're ever going to get unshrunk."

Gaspar put a hand on Albert's nonhumpy shoulder. "You are correct, as usual, old friend."

I glanced uneasily at Sarah, then said, "I'm afraid there's a small problem."

"Of course there's a problem," said Gaspar wearily. "This is life. There's *always* a problem. Well, what is it this time?"

When Sarah blurted out the answer—"They're going to start tearing down Morley Manor tomorrow morning!"—all five little monsters began to carry on something awful. Melisande's snakes had a hissy fit. Ludmilla turned into an inch-long bat and fluttered around like a moth at a candle. Gaspar put his arm to his brow like some tragic hero. "O grim and unrelenting world!" he cried, tipping back his head. "That a man's home should be so easily wrenched from his grasp. Does evil never take a holiday? Does sorrow never cease its sordid work?"

"Don't worry, boss, you'll think of something,"

said Albert. At the same time, Bob howled a tiny, piteous howl.

"Oh, stop!" said Sarah at last. "If it's that important, we'll take you back tonight."

"We will?" I asked in surprise.

"We *have* to, Anthony," said Sarah, her voice urgent. "They need our help."

I realized she was right. Tonight was the last chance the monsters would have to get back to their regular size.

On the other hand, I wasn't sure that having them get big again was such a good idea. Did we really want five full-size monsters running around Owl's Roost?

As if he had read my mind, Gaspar said, "Not only is it the only way for us to return to our regular size, it is the only way for us to return home and— what is the phrase?—get out of your hair."

Melisande's snakes hissed in agreement.

This confused me. "I thought this was where you lived. I mean, here in Owl's Roost. Or do you mean back to your own time?"

"Our other home," hissed Melisande's snakes. "Beyond the Sssstarry Door."

"What's the Starry Door?" asked Sarah.

"Never mind that now," snapped Gaspar, giving Melisande a dark look. "If we don't get back to

Morley Manor before they tear it down, we'll be stuck at this size. Forever."

"And ve vill haf to stay vith you," added Ludmilla, who had morphed back to her human shape. Then she licked her lips and grinned in a way that made me very uncomfortable.

Ludmilla's grin settled it. While it might be cool to have the monsters around for a while, I didn't think I wanted it to be a permanent situation. Who knew how long Ludmilla could control herself?

But as much as I wanted to help them—not to mention get them out of the house—I was still a little nervous about what might happen when they got back to full size.

"Uh—if we do help you get big, you won't eat us, or drink our blood, or anything like that, will you?" I asked nervously.

Gaspar was outraged. "What kind of people do you think we are?" he cried, his eyes blazing.

I spread my hands. "I don't have the slightest idea!"

Ludmilla put a hand on Gaspar's shoulder and whispered in his ear. I could see him relax a little. Turning to me, he said, "My apologies for my outburst. Your concern is not unfounded. Let us see if we can reduce it a bit. Family! Assemble!"

Quickly all five monsters got in a line. Placing his clenched fist over his heart, Gaspar said, "In return for your assistance, we pledge to you—" He paused, then looked at us curiously. "What are your names, please?"

"I'm Anthony Walker. And this is my sister, Sarah."

Gaspar nodded solemnly. "In return for your assistance, we pledge to you, Anthony Walker and Sarah Walker, our friendship, our support in time of need, our sacred honor, and our hope for a better tomorrow. Thus speaks the Family Morleskievich!"

"Thus speaks the Family Morleskievich!" shouted the rest of them (except Bob, of course).

Then all five monsters made a deep bow in our direction. I noticed that Gaspar managed to keep from bumping his nose this time.

"Morleskievich?" asked Sarah.

"Our name before we came to America," said Gaspar. "We only use it for our most serious oaths."

Well, they could have been lying. But we decided to believe them.

It wasn't as if we had much choice.

"We have to go get dressed," I said.

"We will wait for you here," said Gaspar.

I opened the door to the hallway. To my horror, Mr. Perkins came bounding into the room. I tried to catch him, but missed.

Hissing and snarling, the vicious monkey headed straight for our tiny friends.

5

Gaspar's Story

 WHAT HAPPENED NEXT happened very fast. "Family Morleskievich, prepare for battle!" cried Gaspar.

Instantly, Ludmilla turned back into a bat. She flew toward Mr. Perkins and began to dive-bomb his head, causing him to shriek in concern. At the same time, Bob the werehuman dropped into a crouch and began snarling in a truly frightening fashion.

Even more astonishing was the way that Gaspar turned his back to Mr. Perkins and dropped to one

44

knee. Albert came running toward him, put one foot in Gaspar's cupped hands, and next thing I knew was flying through the air, right toward Mr. Perkins. He landed on the monkey's stomach and began climbing up his chest. Mr. Perkins, shrieking in dismay, tried to paw the tiny hunchback off, but Ludmilla kept distracting him.

Only Melisande didn't join in the battle. "You sssshouldn't be sssso mean to him," hissed her snakes, which were tangling around themselves in their excitement.

"Survival first, kindness second!" roared Gaspar. He turned back to Mr. Perkins and began snapping at his toes with his lizardy head.

The monkey had had enough. Turning, he barreled out of the bathroom and down the hall, shrieking as he went. For a second I was afraid he had taken Albert with him. Then I saw the hunchback's fierce little face peering around the edge of the door, so he must have jumped off when Mr. Perkins decided to flee.

"Well done, family!" said Gaspar.

"I sssstill think it wassss mean," said Melisande's snakes. Letting them do the speaking left her free to make a pouty face.

"I thought it was great!" I said. "That monkey's been a bully since the day he got here. It's about time someone taught him a lesson."

"Pleased to be of service," said Gaspar. "Now, if you would be so kind as to conduct us to our home?"

"We still have to get dressed," I said.

Gaspar nodded. "A sensible choice. Man should not face the elements without proper protection."

"Do you think we should wake up Gramma?" asked Sarah.

I made my *yeah, right!* face at her.

She sighed. "I guess you're right. Only it's kind of scary to think about going alone."

"You von't be alone," said Ludmilla. "You'll haf us!"

"And it's not like anyone lives there now," I said, trying to sound braver than I felt.

"I wouldn't necessarily count on *that,*" muttered Gaspar.

"What's that supposed to mean?" I asked sharply.

He shrugged. "Our world is vast and strange, Anthony. Our world is vast and strange."

"Brother issss a bit of a philossssopher," hissed Melisande, gazing at him lovingly.

THE CLOCK on the kitchen wall said 11:45.

Gramma Walker was snoring quietly in her bedroom.

Mr. Perkins glared at us from his perch in the corner of the kitchen, clearly nervous about the weird little creatures that had invaded the house.

And Sarah and I were dressed and ready to head for Morley Manor.

Before we left, we divided the monsters between us. Albert was riding in the right pocket of my yellow raincoat, Bob in the left. Ludmilla and Melisande were riding with Sarah. As for Gaspar, he was sitting on my collar, clinging to my ear to help him keep his balance.

"Ready?" I asked.

"Ready," said Sarah, though the quaver in her voice made it clear she still wasn't sure about this.

"Ready," said Gaspar.

We stepped outside. The rain had stopped, but that appeared to be a temporary situation; dark clouds hid any sign of the stars and moon, and thunder was rumbling ominously in the distance.

"So much for finding out whether Bob should have returned to his own shape or not," muttered Gaspar, glancing up at the pitch-black sky.

It felt weird to have Gaspar clinging to my ear like that, but the position allowed him talk to me, and as we slogged through the wet streets, he began telling me his story. Sarah moved closer, and he shouted a bit so that she could hear, too.

"I was born in Transylvania," he started, "nearly a century ago. I was the second of a set of twin boys. My brother, Martin, beat me into the world by thirteen minutes and thirteen seconds.

"In those days Martin and I were identical not only in face but in feeling. Our minds and our hearts were as one. We thought the same thoughts, felt the same feelings. And the thing we felt most strongly of all was curiosity.

"One evening in the summer of our twelfth year—both our sisters had been born by then, though Melisande was still but a toddler—Martin and I scaled the wall of an ancient, half-ruined castle that stood a mile from our village."

Lightning streaked down in the distance, and Gaspar paused to let the thunder rumble past us before he continued his story.

"The castle was said to be haunted. Martin and I set out to prove that it was not, though we half hoped that it was. We had told our parents we were going to be camping for the night. Our real plans were more daring. I doubt either of us would have attempted such a thing on our own. But together we would try anything, no matter how foolhardy.

"We spread our blankets on the floor of the great hall. As night fell, we heard strange rustlings and stirrings. We tried to explain them away—rats in the walls, the wind coming through a broken window. But then we heard, coming from below us, a moan that was unmistakably human—or at least something like a human."

I shivered, and noticed that Sarah and I were

walking closer together than we had been a minute earlier.

"'Are you ready for this, brother?' asked Martin.

"'I'm at your side,' I affirmed.

"Martin always took the lead in this way, claiming it was his right as elder, a fact that sometimes annoyed, sometimes comforted me. But when it was time to move, we always went together.

"Side by side, we descended the castle stairs, searching for that moaning. Suddenly Martin grabbed my arm. We stopped. In the darkness ahead of us loomed a tall, robed figure—not solid, not real flesh, but seeming to be just a milky glow. It reached out to us, and the sight sent autumn leaves whirling through my heart."

Gaspar fell silent for a moment, lost in his memories.

"Who was it?" demanded Sarah. "What did you do?"

"My first thought was to flee. I probably would have, had I not had Martin at my side. Together, we stood our ground. 'What do you want, strange spirit?' asked Martin."

"Why did you think it wanted anything at all?" I asked.

"Ghosts *always* want something," said Sarah knowingly. "Otherwise they would just move on."

"Precisely," said Gaspar. "This spirit, as if freed

to speak by Martin's question, told us it was a wizard named Wentar. His unhappy shade was imprisoned in the castle halls as punishment for his misdeeds in life." He paused, then added in a bitter voice, "I have since learned that this was not the complete truth."

We heard a car coming, and ducked behind some bushes to hide. Its wheels hissed on the wet street, and it sent up a spray of water as it passed.

"Anyway," Gaspar continued, once the car was gone, "Wentar asked for our aid in freeing his soul from its curse. Martin and I were glad to give that help, for it seemed like a grand adventure. However, the task he assigned us—finding and retrieving a huge jewel called 'The Heart of Zentarazna'—turned out to be more terrifying than we could have imagined."

"What did you have to do to get it?" asked Sarah eagerly.

"It's a long story," said Gaspar, "and I don't have time to give you all the details right now. Let it be enough to say that in order to free him, we had to use a book hidden in a secret library in the castle's eastern tower." He chuckled. "When Wentar told us how to enter that well-concealed room, I do not think he suspected how Martin and I would react to those books. He had offered us gold for our help, but the real reward was the books themselves."

"Why?" asked Sarah, stepping around a deep puddle. "Didn't you have any of your own?"

"We had plenty of books," said Gaspar. "Our father was a great scholar. But these books—ah, these books were filled with ancient and forbidden wisdom, the kind of secrets my twin and I had dreamed of finding, had spoken of in low whispers late at night, but had never truly believed we could possess. Oh, how those pages fired our imaginations! What strange paths of discovery they led us to!"

"Sounds exciting," I said enviously.

Gaspar sighed. "It was. But there is a reason much of that knowledge is forbidden. Soon Martin and I were tampering with forces far beyond our comprehension, walking an edge of danger that we barely understood. Then one night Martin fell through a hole in the world."

"Huh?" I said, not very intelligently.

"It was the most terrifying moment of my life," said Gaspar, his voice heavy. "Worse, even, than the first instant when we saw Wentar. It happened one midnight when Martin and I were in the forest, tracing a maze in the center of a clearing. It was stupid of us; the magic we were playing with was far beyond our understanding. But we had talked ourselves into thinking it was a good idea. This is a specialty of teenage boys. Martin, who always insisted on going first, was walking the path ahead of me. I followed, holding a lantern. All of a sudden I heard him cry out. Then, in an instant, he disappeared—just vanished, right before my eyes.

"I was terrified—and frozen by uncertainty. Should I keep walking the maze, so that I would follow wherever he had gone? Should I wait for him? Should I run for help? I called his name over and over, but there was no answer, no sound at all save that of the wind whispering through the trees above me."

Gaspar's voice was heavy now. "I have never known if it was wisdom or cowardice that kept me from taking those next steps along the maze. Nor do I know how long I stood there, unable to turn back for fear I would break the spell and ruin Martin's chance of returning, unable to move forward for fear I would disappear myself. I only know it was long enough for my body to ache with the effort of holding still, yet not long enough for morning to come.

"Finally, in a burst of green light, Martin did return. He was Martin, yet not Martin, for something about him was different. His spirit was darker. Sorrow colored his eyes. And of what had happened, where he had been, he would not speak at all. As time went on that reticence grew; where once there had been no secrets between us, now there were many. I no longer knew his heart as once I had.

"Despite this horrifying experience, we did not cease our visits to the castle library. If anything, Martin was more eager than ever to continue our investigations. They were thrilling. Yet my heart was heavy, for my twin and I were never again as close as we once had been. The years rolled by. We grew stronger and bolder in our knowledge. Albert came to work for us, which is a story in itself. Our family prospered. When our parents died, Martin and I took on the care of Ludmilla and Melisande. The war came, and we survived that. Then, shortly after peace arrived, Martin decided we should move to America.

"'Something terrible is coming,' he kept saying. 'An evil almost beyond imagination.' He was right, of course. The communists came, and a grayness descended on our homeland."

Gaspar fell silent, and I could sense that he was fighting back painful feelings. He was about to continue his story when we turned down Willow Street.

Ahead, rising against the darkness, dark clouds massed behind it, was Morley Manor. A streak of lightning sizzled out of the sky, illuminating its rickety towers.

"Home," said Gaspar, and in his voice was such love and anger that it frightened me.

6

The Five
Little Monsters
and How They Grew

THE GATE TO MORLEY MANOR was about twelve feet tall and had fierce spikes on the top. I was afraid it would be locked, but I guess the new owner figured that since the place was going to be torn down, there was no point in bothering to keep people out. Or maybe he just figured that no one with a brain in his head would go in there, anyway.

When I tried to open the gate, I realized there was another reason not to bother with a lock: The hinges were so badly rusted that I couldn't budge the thing. I wondered how they had gotten it open for the sale.

"Sarah," I grunted. "Give me a hand with this."

She came up beside me. I looked at her and nodded. We clutched the wet metal bars and began to push with all our might. Suddenly the gate lurched forward about a half a foot, letting out a terrible screech as it did.

The rain was starting again, and, of course, we couldn't hold our umbrella while we were pushing. I shook my head to get the water out of my eyes and said, "Again!"

Another screech, nearly lost in a rumble of thunder from overhead, and the gate lurched open just far enough for us to squeeze through if we turned sideways.

My hair was soaked, and I wished that I had bothered to put up the hood on my raincoat the way Sarah had. Gaspar was soaked, too, so at least I wasn't alone. Bob and Albert, on the other hand, had ducked under the flaps on my pockets and so they stayed dry. It was weird to feel them moving around—almost as if I had a hamster in each pocket.

Lightning crackled through the sky as we started up the walk. Thunder boomed and crashed. I expected Sarah to say she wanted to go home, but she didn't. I think having the monsters with us made us both feel braver. Spooky as Morley Manor was, it seemed like a natural home for our new friends. And since we were here to do them a favor, it somehow felt safe.

It was a relief to get up on the porch and out of the rain. The front door was unlocked, too, and opened much more easily than the gate had. As we stepped inside, a clock began to strike midnight.

"That's weird," said Sarah nervously.

"What?" I asked, barely able to get the word past the dryness in my throat.

"There aren't any clocks here. I watched a lady buy them all this morning."

I shivered.

We let the monsters out of our pockets. The furniture was almost all gone—sold or hauled away—but we found a wobbly table where we could set them. Then Sarah swung her flashlight around the room.

Melisande started to cry. "Our beautiful housssse," she hissed, clutching Ludmilla's arm. "Oh, ssssister, look what hasssss happened to our beautiful housssse."

The snakes on her head drooped mournfully.

Ludmilla patted her on the shoulder, but her lip was trembling and she looked as if she were about to cry, too.

Gaspar just looked angry.

Sarah and I knelt in front of the table so we could talk to them.

"What next?" I whispered.

"We climb the forbidden stair," said Gaspar.

"I should have guessed," I muttered. "All right, where is it?" Remembering the roped-off stairway I had seen that morning, I said, "Never mind, I think I know. You guys wanna walk or ride?"

They decided to walk, so we put them gently on the floor—except for Ludmilla, who turned into a bat again and flew instead.

The sign saying ABSOLUTELY NO ONE PAST THIS POINT was still in place. "What's up there?" I asked when we stood at the base of it.

"My laboratory," said Gaspar. "At least, I hope it's still there." He sounded a little nervous.

"And the Sssstarry Door," hissed Melisande's snakes.

The stairs were too high for the monsters to climb, so Sarah and I picked them up again—except for Ludmilla, who was still flying. Swallowing hard, we started toward the top. Suddenly something crashed below us, so loud and hard that I cried out and nearly stumbled.

"What was that?" screamed Sarah.

"Just the house," said Gaspar, from his perch on my shoulder. When it was clear that we didn't understand, he added, "It makes sounds all by itself."

I could feel my eyes bulge. "What's *that* supposed to mean?"

"Just don't open any doors vithout asking us first," whispered Ludmilla, who was driving me nuts by fluttering around a few inches from my head.

Suddenly a cold wind whistled past us, as if someone had opened an upstairs window.

Sarah shivered. "Where did *that* come from?"

"It's just the house," said Gaspar again.

"Maybe you guys should go the rest of the way on your own," I suggested, stopping a few feet from the top.

"We can't open the laboratory door when we're only five inchessss high!" hissed Melisande, sounding as if she thought I was some sort of idiot.

I sighed and walked on.

All too soon we were at the top of the stairs.

Sarah lifted her flashlight.

A long hallway stretched ahead of us. Several doors opened off from it. At the end of the hallway was a bookcase.

"Okay," I said. "Which door?"

"None of them," said Gaspar.

"But you said—"

"We don't use the doors," said Gaspar. "We use the bookcase. Take out the second book from the right on the fourth shelf."

We walked down the long hall. I pulled out the book. Instantly the whole bookshelf slid up, disappearing into the ceiling.

"It's like a metaphor," said Gaspar smugly. "The bookshelf is the true door to greater knowledge."

I didn't know about greater knowledge, but this was definitely a greater hallway. It stretched ahead of us for an absurd length, clearly going far past the walls of Morley Manor. I couldn't see all the way to the end of it; after about a hundred yards or so, it was shrouded in mist.

"This is too weird," said Sarah.

"On the contrary," said Ludmilla, who had turned back into human form and was sitting on Sarah's shoulder. "It's just weird enough!"

"Take the third door on the right," said Gaspar.

The floor creaked beneath our feet. The door groaned and complained as I pushed it open.

By the light of Sarah's flashlight, I saw what appeared to be a mad scientist's laboratory crossed with a wizard's hideaway. The room looked like no one had entered it in fifty years. The walls were so high I figured the original ceiling must have been taken out so that the room could extend up to include the attic. Or maybe not. Given the hall we had just traveled, it was hard to be sure *how* this place was built.

Medical tables stood side by side with tall wooden stands that held thick, ancient books bound in leather and stamped with titles written in some strange alphabet. The shelves were filled with test tubes, beakers, and green glass bottles with labels like EYE

OF NEWT, POWDERED BAT WING, and TOASTED TOAD TOES. Dust lay thick over everything. Nets of cobwebs stretched from table to shelf, from shelf to floor.

On the far side of the room, on a raised area almost like a little stage, stood five glass cylinders, each about seven feet high.

"Thank goodness they're still here!" cried Gaspar when he spotted the cylinders. "That's where we will be enlarged."

I felt a rustling in the pockets of my raincoat. "Let us out!" cried Albert.

Sarah and I found an empty table. I took Albert and Bob out of my pockets, then took off the raincoat. Sarah set Ludmilla and Melisande on the table beside them, then took off her raincoat, too.

"All right," said Gaspar. "Let's get busy. You will have to operate the controls, Anthony."

"What are you going to use for power?" I asked. "The electricity has been cut off."

"We don't have to fly kites to catch lightning or anything, do we?" asked Sarah nervously.

Gaspar laughed. "There are many other sources of power in this world. See that metal box over there, the one on the table near the center of the room? Take me to it, please."

The box had a glass top, and I could see, through a layer of dust and cobwebs, that it held an enormous green jewel.

"This is The Heart of Zentarazna," said Gaspar. "The jewel I told you of."

"I thought you gave it back to Wentar," I said, staring at it in awe.

"We did. We later earned it back from him. Another story altogether. Place it in the control box over there."

Nervously, I took the jewel from its container. Though it was smooth as glass, it seemed to pulse with energy. When I closed my hands over it, I could see a green glow through my fingers. I placed it gently in the control box.

"Now throw that switch," said Gaspar, pointing to a lever as big as my arm.

I did as he directed. The five glass chambers rose about seven feet into the air.

Albert shouted in triumph, which started Bob howling. With Ludmilla fluttering excitedly around our heads, we carried the other four monsters to the raised area. Eagerly they took their places, one beneath each glass chamber.

When they were all ready, Gaspar said, "Now return the switch to the original position. When the chambers have lowered and been sealed, press the three buttons next to it—first the red one, then the green one, then the black one."

I did as he directed. As soon as I had pushed the third button, a thick green mist began to fill the chambers. Thunder shook the sky outside. Rain pounded against the roof.

Suddenly a crackle of energy filled the room, so strong and intense that Sarah and I both cried out. When I reached for her hand, a bolt of green power shot between us.

"Look!" she cried.

The monsters were getting bigger—slowly at first, then faster and faster. Soon they were taller than us (except for Albert, of course).

Gaspar waved his fists in triumph.

I wondered if it was going to be a good idea to let them out of the chambers. The choice was out of my hands. The glass cylinders lifted on their own.

"Big!" cried Gaspar in a deep baritone voice. "We're big again! Now is the evil spell reversed. Now are we ourselves once more."

Albert leaped to the floor and began to caper about the room. Ludmilla swirled her cape and transformed herself into a bat that had a wingspan of at least three feet. Melisande's snakes nearly tied themselves into knots, they were so excited. Bob threw back his head and howled with joy.

"Ah, my young friends, the Family Morleskievich is deeply in your debt," said Gaspar, stepping toward me.

I know he meant to be friendly, but now that he

was over six feet tall, his lizard head was terrifying. I took a step backward. Sarah moved closer to me.

Gaspar stopped and smiled, showing about four thousand teeth. "I understand your reluctance for me to approach," he said. "Very well. You may be on your way."

The five monsters gathered in a half circle. "You have done the Family Morleskievich a great service," said Gaspar. "We thank you." Then they all made that same sweeping bow they had made when they pledged us their friendship.

Sarah and I headed for the door. To my surprise, I felt a little sad at the idea of leaving. But I was proud, too. We had helped the monsters.

My sorrow and pride lasted until I opened the door.

"Yikes!" cried Sarah. "Who's *that*?"

7

A Wentar's Tale

 THE MANLIKE BEING standing at the door was tall—taller than Gaspar—and dressed in a dark blue robe. At his side hung a leather pouch. His pale face, peering from beneath the shadows of a hood, was long and lined. His dark purple eyes were the most frightening things I had ever seen. Even so, he looked *almost* human.

Almost, but not quite.

Sarah and I took a step back.

"Is it really you, Wentar?" cried Gaspar. His red

tongue flicked in and out between his two-foot-long jaws.

I blinked. What was the ghost of a Transylvanian wizard doing here in Owl's Roost, Nebraska?

The being—I still didn't know if he was a man, a ghost, a wizard, or something else altogether—stepped into the room without answering.

"Where have you been all these years?" demanded Gaspar.

Now Wentar did speak, his voice as rich and deep as a church organ. "What I have been doing since I last saw you is a long story, and one I don't really want to tell right now. We have little enough time as it is if we are going to rescue your brother."

"Martin is dead," said Gaspar, his voice heavy. Then he glanced at me and Sarah and wrinkled his long, lizardy nose. "At least, that is what I have been told."

"What you have been told and what is true are not necessarily the same thing," replied Wentar.

"You vicked children lied to us!" cried Ludmilla. Turning toward me, she bared her fangs and hissed. Now that she was a foot taller than me, this gesture was considerably more frightening than when she had been only four inches high.

"Do not be foolish, Ludmilla," rumbled Wentar. "I was listening. Anthony and Sarah told you the truth as they knew it. The one who lied to you was Martin—or, to be more specific, the being that your family believed was Martin."

Gaspar's eyes grew wide. "Martin was a changeling?" he cried in astonishment.

"Not as you use the word," said Wentar. "Not a goblin creature, or anything such as that—though he was certainly left in place of your brother, just as in the old stories. And yet, in a strange way, he really *was* your brother."

"You're not making much ssssennnsssse," hissed the snakes on Melisande's head. They were writhing and twisting, and I realized that the more upset she was, the more active they got.

"I'm making perfect sense," replied Wentar. "The problem is that *you* are operating on insufficient in formation."

"Then give us more," growled Albert. The wild-eyed hunchback was crouched beside Gaspar, clinging to the edge of his lab coat. I got the impression he didn't particularly like Wentar.

Gaspar shook his enormous head. "Wentar never *gives* information, Albert," he said, a trifle bitterly. "You know there is always a price involved."

"Where I come from information is the preferred form of money," said Wentar. Then he sighed and added, "Alas, where I come from, there is also no doubt that I owe the Family Morleskievich a debt larger than one of my kind should ever owe anyone. So you already have some information coming to you, Gaspar—prepaid, as it were. However, we shall have to be quick. We must be out of here and through the Starry Door before morning comes. Now, what do you want to know?"

Gaspar hesitated just a moment. Then, with a sly look on his lizardy face, he said, "Tell me what I *need* to know."

Wentar smiled, which made it look as if some invisible fingers were pulling up the sags of his pale, droopy face. "Oh, very good! You've learned a lot since last I saw you."

"I've suffered a lot since last you saw me."

Wentar shrugged. "The two things often go together. All right, gather round. Quickly! There is much to be done, not much time to do it, and some things you *do* need to know before we act. I assume, by the way, that you have told the others of all that passed between us back in the old country, Gaspar?"

Gaspar nodded—an interesting effect now that his snout was at least two feet long. Gesturing to me and Sarah, he said, "And I have given these youngsters a quick version of the story."

Wentar glanced at us, and a troubled expression crossed his face. "It would be best to send you two home immediately," he muttered.

Before I could protest that I wanted to stay and

hear his story, he added, "However, I fear the danger is too great for you to leave Morley Manor at this moment"—which made me want to get out of there immediately.

"What danger?" asked Sarah, stepping closer to me.

Wentar lowered his voice. "You are not the only ones out and about tonight. Others are near, including a group that does not wish well to the Family Morleskievich . . . or any of its friends."

I was tempted to say that we weren't really friends of the monsters, since we had just met them a couple of hours ago. But that seemed rude, not to mention potentially dangerous. Besides, I really did feel as if they were our friends.

"Come first light and you two will be safe," said Wentar soothingly. "Until then—better you should stay with us."

Gaspar made an impatient sound. "Tell us what we need to know, Wentar. Quickly!"

Wentar sighed. "Well, the first thing you need to know is that Wentar is not my name. It is the title for what I do. I am *a* Wentar. One of many."

I glanced at Gaspar. His yellow eyes blinked rapidly. Now that he was big, I noticed that the pupils were vertical, like a cat's. In a sorrowful voice he said, "Truth reveals itself in layers, and those you think you know may hide worlds beneath their words. All right, my old teacher, you have my attention. What is a Wentar?"

The Wentar opened his palms, as if to show he had nothing to hide. "A little bit of this, a little bit of that. An explorer. An observer. A reporter. A listener. A judge, sometimes. Primarily . . . an admissions officer."

"But not a wizard," I said. I had a feeling I knew where this was going. Even so, I was surprised to realize that the words had come from me. I had thought I was too scared to speak.

"Not a wizard," agreed the Wentar. "Though I do have some magic at my command. I suppose the most likely term would be . . . an *alien*. I work for the Coalition of Civilized Worlds."

The monsters murmured in surprise. "You mean, as in from another planet?" demanded Albert. "Oy, I should have guessed."

"Why did you not tell me this before?" asked Gaspar. He sounded angry, and a little hurt, as if he felt he had been betrayed.

"When first we met, it was not a time and a place where that idea would have made sense to you," replied the Wentar. "You and Martin were expecting a ghost. And given the nature of my imprisonment— due to my own foolishness I had been caught halfway between your world and mine—a ghost was very much what I seemed." He closed those strange purple eyes for a moment, then said, "At the time, the true nature of my being was not information I was willing to sell to a pair of overactive teenage boys."

Gaspar started to say something, but the Wentar cut him off. "Enough questions. What you need to know *now* is this: The night that you and Martin were foolishly walking a maze and he fell through a hole in the world, he was caught and held prisoner."

"How could he have been held prisoner?" asked Gaspar. "He came back before the sun had risen."

"I am well aware of that," said the Wentar, raising his hands as if to hold off the objection. "What *you* are not aware of is that time passes differently in different worlds—differently enough that in Flinduvia, the world Martin entered, they were able to make a clone of him. That clone is what they sent back here."

"Vat is a clone?" asked Ludmilla.

"An exact copy," replied the Wentar.

Ludmilla bared her fangs. "Vat a stupid idea! Vun of Martin vas more than enough."

"That may well be," said the Wentar. "But the Flinduvians wanted to keep the original."

"For what purposssse?" asked Melisande.

"They wanted to study him," said the Wentar. "To get even more information, they loaded the clone with a copy of Martin's personality, then programmed in some additional instructions of their own and returned it to Earth. The clone was to observe and send back data—much as I do myself, though for considerably different reasons. So if Martin seemed to be the same and yet not the same after his return, it is because that was the exact situation. He was a perfect reproduction of your brother, with some additional . . . programming."

Sarah looked at me nervously, and I could tell she was wondering what it would be like to have a brother like that.

"Why are you telling us this now?" asked Gaspar.

"I have only recently worked it all out myself," said the Wentar. "Also, I am concerned because the Flinduvians have called the clone home."

"Called him home," I repeated. "Does that mean that Old Man . . . er, *Mr.* Morley didn't actually die a few months back?"

"Precisely," said the Wentar. "The Flinduvians sent yet another clone—an empty one, this time; just a well-aged body with nothing in it—and used it to replace the first clone. Now we must try to find the real Martin."

"To save him?" asked Gaspar eagerly, his long, lizardy tongue flicking in and out of his snout.

"Saving Martin would be nice," said the Wentar.

"Certainly it would help ease my conscience. However, the main thing I need to do right now is find out what the Flinduvians are up to, and I think there is a good chance I can do that by tapping Martin's brain."

"But why did they send a clone of him here to begin with?" I asked. "What were they after?"

"I should think *that* much would be obvious," replied the Wentar. "They want to take over your planet."

8

The Starry Door

"WHY WOULD THE FLINDUVIANS want to take over Earth?" I cried. (I suppose that wasn't a particularly sensible question. It just popped out.)

"The other Wentars and I have often asked ourselves the same thing," replied the purple-eyed alien. "Considering the mess you people have made of this place, it's hard to imagine why anyone would want it. Of course, the planet's basic structure is still sound; lots of water and so on. But everyone in the galaxy knows how much work it would take to clean up your world enough to make it suitable for civilized life. So there must be something else. We have some theories, but we still—"

Before he could finish the sentence, he spun as if he had heard something behind him—though what it was I couldn't have said, since I heard nothing but the rain pounding against the windows. When he turned back, his eyes were wide. I wasn't sure it was a look of fear (with an alien, who can tell?) until he whispered, "Quickly! Follow me! The Flinduvians are coming."

The urgency in his voice made it clear: He was terrified—which didn't do anything to calm *me* down, let me tell you.

I glanced at Gaspar to see if he was going to do as the Wentar said.

He was already heading for the door.

"What about the children?" he asked.

"They'll have to come with us," said the Wentar. "We'll try to bring them back later. *Hurry!*"

Sarah grabbed my hand. Normally, I wouldn't have put up with that, but this was not a normal situation. It didn't make any difference. My fingers had barely closed over hers when I felt her hand being yanked out of mine.

"Sarah!" I cried, terrified that the aliens had snatched her. Then I saw what had really happened:

Albert had picked her up and thrown her over his shoulder—the one without the hump. Moving amazingly fast, he scuttled out the door after the Wentar.

Bob the werehuman was close on their heels.

"Hurry, Anthony!" said Ludmilla, just before she turned into a bat and flew after them.

Melisande took my hand. "Sssstay with meeee!" hissed her snakes.

I did just that. Weird as she was, it was better than being alone. The two of us scurried into the hall. We hadn't gone more than twenty or thirty feet when I felt a jolt that reminded me of the time I accidentally touched the electric fence at Gramma and Grampa Walker's farm with my head. Except this time was both less painful and about twenty times more powerful.

"What was that?" I cried.

No one answered. I had a feeling I knew what it meant, anyway. We had crossed some line—a line like the one we had crossed when we first entered the hallway.

Now we were somewhere else.

But *where*?

We kept running. I heard a shout behind us. When I looked over my shoulder, I was so startled that I stumbled and would have fallen if Melisande had not pulled me back to my feet.

Though the corridor stretched behind us, it didn't go all the way back to the stairs, or even back to the place we had stepped through when the bookshelf had lifted out of the way. Instead, it ended at a shimmering wall of black. I figured that must mark the place we had passed when I felt that weird jolt.

Now, to my horror, that black wall began to bulge. Something from the other side was slamming against it. I could hear angry shouts. The blackness seemed to be stretching, getting *thinner*.

Melisande yanked me forward.

"Don't sssstop!" hissed the snakes on her head.

And then we were there. The Starry Door.

There was no mistaking it. It was as black as the wall behind us, as if we were in some sort of long capsule, with a black wall at each end. But unlike the wall we had already come through, which was solid black, this wall was marked with a circle of stars that pulsed with silver light. The Wentar paused, glanced behind us. I heard a shout and turned to look, too.

The wall behind us had been sliced to tatters by thick, glittering claws. But the tatters themselves still had power, because the creature on the other side was struggling with them, trying to get through. I caught a glimpse of a face—large eyes and a bulging purple snout, with big fangs thrusting up from its lower jaw—that was both fierce and frightening.

The creature let out a cry of rage that seemed to scrape along my soul.

"Hurry!" cried Gaspar. "Hurry!"

The Wentar ran his fingers over the circle of stars, touching them in an order I couldn't make out. With a musical shimmer, the door opened, revealing a great black void sprinkled with stars. I expected to be sucked through, destroyed instantly. But as if the stars themselves were only an image on a curtain, the Wentar reached forward and touched one.

"I want to go *there*," he said, speaking to the door. Then he turned to us and said, "Follow me."

He stepped forward. The black void rippled and seemed to swallow him.

Gaspar followed at his heels. Ludmilla went next; fluttering after her brother, she disappeared into the darkness. Then Albert stepped through, with Sarah still flung over his shoulder.

"Wait!" I cried.

It was too late; they were gone.

I glanced behind me. The creature I had seen before was pushing its way through the tattered black ribbons that were all that remained of the barrier. Though they clung to him and tried to hold him back, it was clear he would be free of them in seconds. Behind him were more of his kind, growling and snorting.

Then the monster locked eyes with me. I felt a coldness, and a strange glimpse of terror to come. I stood, frozen, like some helpless prey in the eyes of a great hunting beast.

"We musssst go!" cried Melisande, yanking my hand.

The spell was broken. Turning, I followed her through the Starry Door.

I FELT AS IF I were being stung by a thousand bees and kissed by a thousand butterflies, all at the same time.

My body was still tingling when I realized I was standing in a green field dotted with little red flowers. The moment of comfort I felt when I saw this didn't last very long. Though the field was green, what grew on it was not like any grass I had ever seen. It looked more like a lawn of two-inch-high broccoli. It was the same with the flowers: Though clearly *like* flowers in general, they were just as clearly unlike any flowers I had ever actually seen. (And as the son of two florists, I've seen more than my share of flowers.) The stiff red petals that radiated out from the bumpy centers had a metallic look. I reached down to touch one, then cried out in pain. The edge was so sharp it had cut me, almost like a paper cut.

Putting my bleeding finger in my mouth, I looked up. The sky was as purple as wild irises.

"Anthony," said Sarah uneasily, "we're not in Nebraska anymore, are we?"

"Nor are ve in Zentarazna," said Ludmilla, who had turned back to her human form. She sounded as nervous as I felt—which made *me* even more nervous than I had been to begin with. "Just vere *haf* you brought us, Ventar?"

"To a place where we may be safe—and where we may be able to gather some information."

"What about those . . . *things*?" I asked.

"We are safe from them for now. They cannot follow through the Starry Door. That is the law of magic."

"Good law," said Albert.

The Wentar didn't answer. Instead, he began turning in a slow circle. He was making an odd humming noise in his throat. The noise might have been nervousness. It might have been some secret call. Maybe he was just singing.

As I said, with an alien, who can tell?

Halfway into his second circle, he paused, then pointed. "This way," he said. "Quickly!"

He began striding off across the field. The rest of us followed.

What else could we do?

The grassy stuff felt sproingy under my feet, and I almost bounced as I walked. It made a wonderful sound, too—a humming not unlike the sound the

Wentar had been making. The air was clean and crisp, so sweet to breathe that I couldn't help remembering the Wentar's words about the mess we had made on Earth. I wondered what our own air was supposed to smell like.

After about fifteen minutes, we crested a hill. I could see an enormous lake ahead of us, its blue green surface rippled by gentle waves. As we ambled down the slope toward the sandy shore, something rose up out of the water.

I came to a dead stop.

Sarah grabbed my arm.

"What the heck is *that*?" she cried.

9

Waterguys

THE CREATURE that stood dripping at the edge of the water was about four feet high. Even though it had arms and walked upright, it looked sort of like a cross between a frog and a fish. A spiny crest ran from its head to its butt. Huge, goggling eyes were set above a mouth so wide that I figured if the thing yawned the top of its head would fall off. It had gills, but no scales. Its skin, which glistened in the sunlight, looked like mottled purple leather with a light coating of slime.

I probably should have been more scared than I was. Maybe what kept me from totally wigging out is the fact that I like frogs so much. We have a lot of them around Owl's Roost, and I like to catch them and "hypnotize" them. (It's a trick I learned from a library book. If you turn a frog upside down and slowly rub your fingertip from its throat down along its belly over and over again, pretty soon it will get totally calm and just lie there in your hand, unable to move. It's really cool, but you have to be very gentle when you do it.)

The waterguy held up a webbed hand, then made a series of croaks that sounded like a whole frog orchestra—everything from the tiny trills of spring peepers to something like the rumble of a bullfrog, only much, much deeper.

The Wentar put his hands on the sides of his own neck for a moment, then made a series of similar sounds.

Given the fact that I can barely pass my French tests, I found this very impressive.

The waterguy responded with another froggy chorus.

"What did he say?" asked Gaspar.

"His name is Chug-rug-lalla-apsa-lalla-rugum-bupbup," replied the Wentar, the words coming from deep in his throat. "But you can call him Chuck."

"That's a relief," muttered Albert.

The Wentar glared at him. "Chuck welcomes us, as long as we guarantee that we come in peace."

"A welcome is all very nice," said Gaspar impatiently. "The question is, will he *help* this band of poor lost wanderers?"

"That is what I am trying to find out," snapped the Wentar. "Perhaps if you stop interrupting me, I will be able to get an answer."

Gaspar clamped his mouth shut and demonstrated what a lizard looks like when it feels both embarrassed and angry.

The Wentar and the waterguy talked for another minute or so, sounding like a chorus of swamp creatures on a warm spring night. Finally the Wentar turned to the rest of us and said, "Lie on your backs."

Gaspar looked suspicious. "For what reason?"

The Wentar sighed. "I have to do something, and it will be easier if you are all lying down—preferably in a circle, with your heads at the center."

Gaspar tightened his jaws, then nodded twice—once at the Wentar, once at the rest of us, indicating we should do as he said. It took a while. Albert couldn't get comfortable, because of his hump. And Bob whined and growled, causing Gaspar to admit that they had never managed to train him very well.

For me, the worst of it was the snakes on Melisande's head, which wouldn't hold still. I had just settled in to my spot when one of them came slithering across my neck, causing me to scream and leap to my feet.

"What now?" asked the Wentar angrily.

"Snake!" I gasped, clutching at my neck. "It was crawling over me."

Melisande looked offended, and her snakes all hissed, "He wassssn't going to hurt you. He wassss jusssst checking you out."

Gaspar's tongue, long as a snake itself, flicked in and out of his mouth. "Lie back down," he ordered. "Melisande, keep the boys under control."

She glared at him, but nodded.

"Glad it wasn't me," whispered Sarah when I was on my back again.

"I wish it had been," I said. That was only partly true. I actually kind of like snakes. Sarah hates them, and if one had crawled over *her* neck, it might have taken hours for us to get her settled down again.

The Wentar began to walk around us, muttering in a low voice. He took something from the leather pouch at his side, and sprinkled it over our heads. Then Chug-rug-lalla-apsa-lalla-rugum-bupbup splashed water on us.

"Hold still!" ordered the Wentar when we started to sit up, and he said it so sharply that even Bob obeyed. Then he began to sing in a low voice, gesturing over us as he did. I felt a weird tingle creep across my skin.

After about five minutes, the Wentar said, "*Now* you can sit up."

"What was that all about?" I muttered.

Though I was speaking to myself, Chuck answered me. "We were arranging things so you could communicate with us more easily."

Actually, what he said was a whole series of croaks and peeps. But I understood them perfectly!

"How did *that* happen?" asked Sarah.

She sounded as astonished as I felt.

She also sounded just like Chuck. I don't mean she had his voice, just that the sounds she was making were in his language. I stared at her in amazement.

"We cast a spell on you, of course," said the Wentar.

I had always figured aliens would be superscientific; I was having a hard time getting used to the idea of them as magic users.

"Follow me," said the waterguy, heading for the edge of the lake. "I want you to meet my mother."

"She doesn't mind having strangers just drop by?" I asked nervously.

"Does she live *underwater*?" asked Sarah, sounding even more nervous.

"Don't worry," Chuck said. "You'll be able to breathe. We took care of that, too." He squatted, then sprang forward, not even looking to see if we were going to follow him. The jump carried him a good thirty feet straight out. He landed with a large splash, then disappeared beneath the surface.

The Wentar waded in after him. Bob followed close at his heels, but I suspect that was mostly because he liked the water. Though he was still in his semihuman form, he barked exuberantly as he bounded through the rippling waves. Suddenly he plunged in over his head, as if he had just gone past a drop-off. He came up once, splashing and spluttering, then disappeared again. This time he didn't come back up.

"Must be the breathing thing works," said Sarah.

"Either that, or something ate him," replied Albert.

"Don't be ridiculous," snapped Gaspar. Squaring his shoulders, he waded into the water after Bob, the Wentar, and Chuck. "Come along, Albert," he said, without looking back. "Destiny awaits."

"Whatever you say, boss," said Albert. He glanced back at me and Sarah, rolled his eyes, spread his hands in a what-can-you-do? kind of gesture, then turned and followed Gaspar into the water.

That left Ludmilla, Melisande, Sarah, and me standing on the shore.

"What about my hair?" muttered Melisande.

It wasn't the kind of girl question it sounds like, since her snakes were twisting and writhing around her head in great alarm. Even so, it did make me realize that it was just me and the girls on the beach.

So I stepped in.

"Anthony, wait!" cried Sarah. She came splashing after me.

The water was cold, and had an odd, lemony smell. The smell was actually kind of pleasant, it was just weird. It was also weird to go in with my clothes on. Though the legs of my jeans were already damp from the walk to Morley Manor, now they clung tightly to my skin, feeling cold and heavy. I was glad I hadn't put anything important in my pockets before we left home that night.

As we moved deeper into the lake, I heard Melisande and Ludmilla wade in behind us, grumbling and hissing as they did. I figured they were even unhappier about getting their clothes wet than I was. But I didn't look back. I was busy peering into the water around me, worrying about everything from man-eating plants to giant slime fish to living mud. Given the creature we had already met, who knew what sorts of things might live in the lakes of this planet?

Suddenly Gaspar stuck his head above the surface. Water streamed off his long snout.

"For heaven's sake," he shouted. "Hurry up!"

That was a good sign. The fact that we had not seen any of the others who had gone under had had me worried. Turning to Sarah, I said, "Ready?"

She nodded. Joining hands, we waded forward. Since she was shorter, her head went under first. I stood and watched.

Okay, I know that makes me sound really rotten. But I figured if there was a problem, it would be easier for me to haul her out than vice versa.

A second later she stuck her head up and called, "Hurry, Anthony! This is really neat!"

Then I was annoyed because I hadn't gone under first.

I plunged in after her. I tried holding my breath, but I quickly realized that that couldn't last for long. Besides, the point was to breathe the water. Cautiously—*very* cautiously—I let some of it trickle in through my nose.

Utterly cool! Instead of choking and burning, the water felt good in my lungs.

Feeling bolder, I drew in a deep breath, filling my lungs with lemony water. It was heavy in my chest, but not uncomfortable.

I looked around. The Wentar's spell must have done something to our eyes as well as our lungs, because I could see perfectly. Strange, fishlike creatures swam all around us. Some of them were transparent, like ghost fish; others had big goggling eyes, or fins that trailed behind them like ribbons. Ahead of us weird plants stretched toward the surface, bending back and forth like ghostly, grasping hands. A variety of brilliantly colored flowers, some as small as thimbles, some as big as dinner plates, bloomed on the bottom.

Boy, I bet Mom and Dad would love some of those for the shop, I thought.

Then I spotted Gaspar. He looked impatient.

"Come on," I said to Sarah. "We'd better hurry."

I half expected the words to come out in little bubbles. Duh. You have to have air to make bubbles, and we weren't breathing air anymore. So the words just came out as sound, made odd by the fact that they were traveling through water rather than air.

I glanced over my shoulder. The lake bed sloped up behind us. Ludmilla and Melisande were completely underwater now, too, and Melisande's snakes were writhing wildly about her head. I hoped the snakes were all right. I thought about going back to check, but I figured Melisande would know if anything was wrong. Even as I watched, they began to settle down. Since Melisande didn't turn and head for the surface, I figured they were relaxing, not drowning.

I glanced up. The sun catching on the water that

rippled overhead made the surface look like some kind of silvery ceiling, with a pattern that changed from moment to moment. I tapped Sarah's shoulder and pointed for her to look. She smiled, then said happily, "This is the weirdest, coolest thing that's ever happened to us, Anthony."

I didn't know if she meant breathing underwater, or everything that had gone on since we first put Albert in the sink. Either way, she was right.

Melisande and Ludmilla had caught up with us by that time. "Ve'd better keep moving," said Ludmilla.

We started out again. The lake bed was getting kind of mucky, and some clinging weeds made it hard to walk, so we began to swim, which turned out to be a lot easier.

Though we could breathe, the water was still wet, of course. So our hair was floating around our heads, while our clothes were plastered to our bodies—not that Melisande's dress hadn't been pretty much plastered to her body already. Sarah caught me looking at her now and gave me an elbow in the ribs.

As we swam deeper, I felt the pressure of the water begin to squeeze me. I wondered how far down we were going to go—and whether the Wentar's spell would protect us from being squished by the water's great weight.

I was gazing around, fascinated by the fish and

the scenery and not paying much attention to where we were heading, when suddenly Sarah cried, "Holy mackerel!"

At first I thought she had seen a giant fish. Then I realized that the waterguy had led us over a cliff. I was terrified when I saw that dark drop beneath us, but really, it was no big deal. When you're already in the water you're not going to fall or anything. As my terror began to ebb I studied the strange landscape below us.

Then I saw what Sarah had been shouting about. It wasn't the cliff, after all. My heart began to pound again, and I wondered if we had been betrayed.

10

The Mother
of All Frogs

 SQUATTING IN THE CENTER of that land-
scape, huge and astonishing, was a creature that
looked somewhat like Chug-rug-lalla-apsa-lalla-
rugum-bupbup, with one major difference: This one
was bigger than our house!

When I first saw it, I thought it must be some kind
of statue the waterpeople had made. But seconds after
we cleared the edge of the cliff, the enormous beast
rolled its huge eyeballs in their sockets, looked up at
us, blinked twice, then opened its mouth.

Out shot a tongue that had to be at least a hundred feet long. Like a green ribbon of death, the tongue wrapped around the Wentar and pulled him into the creature's mouth, so fast it was almost as if it hadn't happened.

Panic exploded in my chest. Was this how I was going to die—swallowed by a giant frog on an alien planet?

I looked around frantically for Sarah. She was only a few feet from me. "Come on!" I cried. "Let's get out of here."

I reached for her hand—instinct, I guess, since it was actually a pretty silly thing to do: You can't swim very fast while you're holding hands.

"Wait!" ordered Chug-rug-frogbutt.

Right. Like I was about to wait so he could feed us to his master, or whatever this thing was. But—instinct again?—I did turn my head back. As I did, I saw the Wentar crawl from between the huge creature's lips. He climbed over the tip of its nose until he had found a broad, flat spot where he could stand. Then he motioned for us to swim down and join him.

"Should we do it?" whispered Sarah.

Gaspar, who was floating nearby, said, "Once again we find the universe is stranger than we could have guessed. What new things shall we discover in this watery world? Forward, my family. Forward."

Which pretty much decided things for the Morleys. As for me, I figured if we tried to swim away the monster would probably just nail us with its tongue anyway. So I nodded to Sarah. "Come on," I said. "Let's go."

We swam deeper into the mysterious lake.

"This is Queen Gunk-alla-gunk-gunk-ipsim-alla-ribit," explained the Wentar when all seven of us had joined him on the creature's snout.

"She is the mother of us all," added Chuck.

"Speak for yourself," said Albert.

"She is also my official contact here," continued the Wentar, casting a dark glance at the little hunchback. "And our best chance for solving our problem. We need to go inside to talk to her."

"Inside where?" I asked, looking around for a building, and wondering how big it would have to be to hold this monster.

"Her mouth," said the Wentar.

"You haf got to be kidding!" cried Ludmilla.

Melisande's snakes twisted in alarm.

"Humor is not one of my specialties," said the Wentar. "Now follow me. We are being treated with extreme kindness by an incredibly powerful being. It would not be wise to make a fuss about it."

Stretching his arms, he swam off the frogmonster's snout. Chuck went with him, not even looking back. The rest of us stood for a moment, baffled, astonished, and terrified. Then Gaspar threw back his shoulders. "Family Morleskievich!" he barked. "Assemble!"

Quickly the monsters got in a line.

"We are the Family Morleskievich," said Gaspar solemnly. "We do not flinch from danger. We do not shy from the unknown. I say we go forward!"

"Forward!" cried the others.

"Forward!" I cried, unable to help myself.

Which is how Sarah and I ended up following the Morleys over the edge of the queen's giant snout.

We hadn't been off the frogmonster's nose for more than three seconds when her great mouth opened and a rush of water pulled us into a dark space—a space that got even darker when the mouth closed again.

This time I was sure we were done for. But a second later the Wentar did some of his magic, and a dim light blossomed around us.

The inside of the queen's mouth was slightly smaller than my bedroom. Her tongue looked like a spongy shag rug. Sarah and I drifted down to stand on it, as the others were doing. I was relieved to find it was not as sticky and slimy as I had feared.

Toward the rear of her mouth I saw a pair of bulges, which I finally realized must have been the back of her eyeballs. Beyond those bulges was the vast darkness of her throat—something I didn't intend to get anywhere near, if I could help it.

Suddenly a deep thrum filled the air around us. It took me a moment to realize that the sounds were words—huge, booming words. Later the Wentar explained that the queen formed them by making a very tiny (for her) rumble in her throat.

"Greetings to the Wentar of Ardis and his companions."

"Greetings to Queen Gunk-alla-gunk-gunk-ipsim-alla-ribit," replied the Wentar. "And our thanks to you for the sheltering warmth of your mouth. May your progeny ever increase, and your children number in the millions."

"They do already," replied the queen, sounding somewhat tired. "Two million, four hundred and thirteen thousand, five hundred and seventy-nine, to be precise."

"Madam, you outdo yourself!" said the Wentar admiringly.

"I undo myself," she replied. "Now, let us get down to business, Wentar. I understand you are involved with that messy little planet called Earth."

"Indeed I am," replied the Wentar. "In fact, I have seven of its people with me on this trip."

I thought it was nice of him to count Bob as a person.

"That is highly unusual, is it not?" asked the queen.

"The circumstances were unusual. I have become rather more involved in their affairs than I would like. I brought these young ones with me because we were being pursued."

"Ah," said the queen. "Let me guess. The Creatures of the Red Haze?"

"Indeed," said the Wentar. He sounded a bit surprised.

"Creatures of the Red Haze?" asked Gaspar. He sounded as confused as the Wentar had sounded surprised.

"It is a name sometimes used for Flinduvians," said the Wentar. "The 'Red Haze' is a condition unique to their species—a kind of anger beyond anger that they sometimes slip into. The results can be . . . remarkable."

"It is not a suitable condition for a civilized being," said the queen.

"Agreed," said the Wentar. "Which is one reason I am monitoring them. I am almost certain they are up to something. Do you have any idea what it is?"

"That I cannot tell you," replied the queen. Before the Wentar could express his disappointment, she added, "However, perhaps one of my children will be able to give you some information."

Suddenly I felt a vibration so powerful that at first

I thought it was an earthquake. Sarah staggered against me. I saw the monsters all crouching, holding on to one another, trying to keep from tumbling over. Then I realized that whatever was going on couldn't be an *earth*quake, because we were standing on a giant tongue.

Was our hostess trying to swallow us?

"What was that?" demanded Gaspar, when the vibration stopped.

"I have sent out the Watercall," replied the queen. "I'm sorry you could not understand it. It will travel many miles. If any of my children have knowledge of this thing, they will come to us." She hesitated, then added, "They have no choice."

"Must be a mom thing," whispered Sarah.

Before five minutes had passed, the queen said, "Ah! A response. I am going to ask you to go outside for the discussion. I grow tired of trying not to swallow."

Once she had said that, she couldn't open her mouth fast enough to suit me.

Together, our little party swam out to meet the creature that had answered the queen's call. He looked enough like Chuck to be his brother. (Which, of course, he was.) He said his name was Unk-lalla-apsa-ribba-ribba-glibbit, then added, "But you can call me Unk."

We found a place to sit next to the queen's left rear foot, which towered over us. Once we Earthlings had introduced ourselves, Unk said, "Mother says you want to know about the Flinduvians."

"That is correct," said the Wentar. "Specifically, what it is that they want with Earth."

"Oh, I know nothing about *that*," said Unk quickly.

I didn't believe him for a second. His eyes were desperate, haunted—as if he was lying not because he wanted to, but because he was afraid to tell the truth.

Chuck saw it, too. "Speak truly, brother," he said fiercely. "I demand it by the bond of our blood."

Unk's eyes rolled back in his head. He shivered, as if taken by a chill. "I know nothing about it," he croaked.

"In your mother's name, I command you to speak!" cried the Wentar.

Unk began to tremble more violently. Suddenly, as if the fear was too much, he turned and started to swim away.

"Catch him!" cried the Wentar.

I was closest. I grabbed Unk's leg. The purple skin was slick beneath my fingers, the leg astonishingly strong. I clung to it with all my might. Though I couldn't stop him by myself, I slowed him enough for the others to grab him. He thrashed wildly.

Suddenly I had an idea. "Turn him on his back!" I shouted.

Gaspar looked startled.

"No!" cried Chuck. "Don't!"

The rest of us looked at him in surprise.

"It's not dignified," he said softly.

I think the others might have ignored my strange request if not for that. But the tension in Chuck's voice made it clear that something about putting Unk on his back had power in it. So despite Chuck's protests, the monsters wrestled Unk to the silty floor of the lake. As they held him down, his arms and legs pinned out straight, I began to stroke his belly, working from the throat down, just as I had done a hundred times with the frogs I caught in the swamp at the edge of Gramma and Grampa's farm. Of course, Unk was so big that I had to use my whole hand, rather than just a fingertip. But the idea was the same.

"You shouldn't do that," said Chuck softly, wringing his webbed hands together. "You shouldn't do that."

Unk blinked his eyes, quickly at first, then more and more slowly. Soon his struggles grew less violent. Gradually, his arms and legs relaxed.

A moment later he was lying limp and still.

"Now is the Wentar of Ardis content?" asked Chuck bitterly.

I stepped back, feeling very clever. "That was really good, Anthony," whispered Sarah.

"Shhhh!" hissed Melisande's snakes.

The Wentar bent over Unk. "Have you been in contact with the Flinduvians?" he whispered.

Without opening his eyes, Unk nodded.

The Wentar looked more sad than angry. Placing his mouth close to the side of Unk's head (the water-guy didn't really have an ear, just a brownish circle), he said urgently, "What do the Flinduvians want with Earth?"

Unk made a sound deep in his throat. Then, as if the words were being dragged from someplace deep within him, he said, "They want Earth's ghosts."

The Wentar blinked. The monsters made watery cries of astonishment. Sarah moved closer to me.

Without intending to, I asked the next question: "What for?"

Unk's answer, which came out almost as a sob, astonished us all.

"They're going to use them for batteries!"

11

Where Is
the Land of the Dead?

GASPAR LEANED close to Unk. Eyes blazing, he hissed, "What do you mean, *batteries*?"

The waterguy swallowed hard, making a deep, ribbity sound. "I do not know the details, only what I overheard. Your ghosts have unusual energy. The Flinduvians plan to use that energy to power a weapon they have invented."

Gaspar's long tongue flicked angrily between his big lizardy jaws. "That is the most immoral thing I have ever heard!"

I had to agree. Using the part of a person that

lives on beyond death, especially using it for a weapon, sounded worse than murder to me. I wondered if it would use up the ghost—kill it. Was that even possible? And if it didn't kill it, what *would* happen to a ghost that was being used for its power?

With a sudden chill, I wondered if Grampa Walker was a ghost now. Was everyone who died a ghost, or was it just people who had unfinished business?

Did *he* have unfinished business?

Suddenly this thing with the Flinduvians seemed very personal.

"How did you learn this?" asked the Wentar. "What is your connection with the Flinduvians?"

"I have accepted a commission to work as their agent on this planet."

Chuck gasped in astonishment. "Does Mother know this?"

"Of course not," whispered Unk, his voice filled with shame.

"What else do you know of their plans?" asked the Wentar. His voice was stern and angry.

"Nothing!" cried Unk. *"Nothing!"*

The Wentar didn't seem to believe this. He asked Unk several more questions, but none of them turned up any new information.

Finally the Wentar made a snort of disgust. "Flip him over," he said.

We did, which instantly broke the hypnotic spell.

I expected Unk to leap to his feet and swim away. But he seemed really frightened of the Wentar now, too frightened to flee. "What are you going to do to me?" he asked, his throat bobbling nervously.

The Wentar smiled, the kind of smile I was glad he was directing at someone else. "I'm not going to do anything," he said softly. "I'll let your mother handle things from here on in."

Unk made a tiny squeaking sound and looked as if he was about to fall down again.

"Take him home," said the Wentar, speaking to Chuck. "Make sure he doesn't have a chance to get any information to the Flinduvians."

"I will be glad to," said Chuck, who had clearly gone from being upset with the way we were treating Unk to being furious with Unk himself.

"Please give your mother my warmest regards, my thanks for her assistance, and my regrets that she has such an unfortunate son as Unk-lalla-apsa-ribba-ribba-glibbit. Tell her I am sure the other two million, four hundred and thirteen thousand, five hundred and seventy-eight are much more a credit to her."

Unk groaned.

"It will be my pleasure," said Chuck.

We watched the two of them swim away.

"Now what?" asked Gaspar, after they had vanished among the seaweed and the fishes.

"We return to the Starry Door as quickly as possible," said the Wentar.

"Are we going home?" I asked eagerly.

"I am not sure," said the Wentar. "Two things need to be done. We must take a warning back to Earth. And we need to investigate what the Flinduvians are up to—hopefully, by regaining Martin. Both tasks are vital."

"It sounds as if we should split up," said Gaspar reluctantly.

"A good idea," agreed Ludmilla. "Ve should not involve the children in this, anyvay."

Part of me was offended. Another part of me was going, *Darn right! Get us out of here!*

The Wentar shook his head. "Anthony and Sarah are already involved. Since the Flinduvians are aware of them, sending them back will not ensure their safety. In fact, it could endanger them. The primary reason to split up is to carry the warning back without delay."

"I don't get it," said Sarah. "Who would we take the warning to? The FBI? The president?"

Gaspar laughed. "These matters are beyond those dreamed of in their thoughts, which are all too tied to the world that they can see. It is unlikely they would believe us, even if we could reach them."

"I dunno," I said. "If the president got a look at

you guys, he'd have to believe almost anything was possible."

"It is good for men of power to haf their assumptions shaken," said Ludmilla smugly.

"Even if your leaders did believe you, they wouldn't know what to do," said the Wentar. "No, we need to get our warning to those most in peril."

"What do you mean?" asked Albert, who had been swimming around, trying to catch a passing fish.

"I should think it would be obvious," said the Wentar. "We need to warn the dead."

Bob began to howl. Melisande's snakes slid around her head uneasily.

"How the heck are we supposed to do *that*?" I asked nervously.

"Someone must make a trip to Earth's Land of the Dead," said the Wentar.

"Land of the Dead?" whispered Sarah. "That sounds pretty scary!"

"How do we get there?" I asked. "It's sure not on the map."

The Wentar turned his huge purple eyes in my direction, and suddenly I wished I hadn't asked the question. What if the only way you could get to the Land of the Dead was by . . . dying?

From the way Melisande's snakes were twisting and writhing, I got a feeling that the same thought had crossed her mind.

"I don't even understand what it means," said Sarah. "What *is* the Land of the Dead?"

The Wentar looked very serious. Actually, with his long face and mournful eyes, he always looked serious. But now he looked even more so.

"It is a world between life and death," he whispered. "A place where the lost and the rebellious, the stubborn and the misguided wait, and plan, and grieve, and mourn. It is not the right place for them to be."

"Then why are they there?" I asked.

The Wentar sighed. "Even though the dead should move on to what is next, not every soul is ready to let go of its previous stage of existence. Various things hold them back—sometimes pain, sometimes anger, sometimes simply unfinished business. Sometimes it is that they cannot let go of those they love. Sometimes, very rarely, it is joy that holds them. The Land of the Dead is a realm of great souls and small, a place that is not a place. Grief runs there like flowing water. Solace, too, though most ignore it. Some souls never see this place. Some stay no more than a day. But others—stubborn, or blind, or in deeper pain than most—may remain for centuries."

I felt a coldness as he spoke, a chill that lingered in my spine long after he was finished.

"How do we get there?" asked Sarah in a hushed voice.

"The easiest way is to die," said the Wentar.

When he saw the look on our faces, he began to chuckle, the first time I had heard him make that sound. "You needn't worry! Just because it is the easiest way does not mean that it is the only way, or even the best. The most likely avenue is actually through a connection. Do any of you know someone who has died recently?"

"Ve haf been locked in a box for fifty years," pointed out Ludmilla. "I suspect *most* of the people ve used to know haf died. But who can guess *ven* they did it?"

"Of coursssse, there wassss Martin," hissed Melisande's snakes.

"But he was not the real Martin," pointed out Gaspar.

"Real or not, it doesn't make any difference," said the Wentar. "Your brother did *not* die. His clone was taken back to Flinduvia and replaced with a replica that had never actually been alive to begin with. That is the body that was buried on Earth; it was dead flesh, nothing else."

"What about you two?" asked Gaspar, turning toward Sarah and me. "Do you know anyone who has not long since slipped the bonds of Earth and laid down his mortal burden?"

"Oh, jeez, boss," said Albert. Turning to us, he

added, "What he means is, do you know anyone who's died lately?"

We did, of course. But I couldn't answer him, couldn't get the words past the lump in my throat.

Sarah answered for me. "There was Grampa," she said slowly.

"When did he die?" asked the Wentar. To my surprise, his voice was sympathetic.

"About three months ago," said Sarah, her voice trembling a little.

"Is it likely he would have been the sort not to move on?" asked Gaspar.

"He *was* stubborn," I said, smiling a bit in spite of myself.

"I bet he's waiting for Gramma," added Sarah. "He never liked to go anywhere without her."

"Then he may be our best ticket," said the Wentar.

I didn't particularly like the idea of Grampa Walker as a "ticket" to the Land of the Dead. But I liked the idea of his soul being used as a battery by some bizarre alien race even less.

"Are you children willing to do this?" asked the Wentar, turning his purple eyes to Sarah and me. "I will not hide the fact that the journey will have its dangers. But the stakes are great, for both the living and the dead of your planet."

I looked at Sarah. Her eyes were wide and frightened. But I knew my little sister well enough to know that just because she was afraid didn't mean she was unwilling to do something. I raised a questioning eyebrow.

Sarah gave me just the slightest nod.

The Family Morleskievich weren't the only ones who had their rituals, their ways of making decisions.

I turned to the Wentar.

"We'll do it."

12

A Family Divided

THE WENTAR had to perform a reverse spell on us when we left the lake, so that we could breathe normally again. Unfortunately, the spell didn't dry us out, so we were dripping and uncomfortable as we slogged our way back across the sproingy broccoli-grass. It was moving on toward night, and a cool evening breeze had come up, which made things even worse.

The only one who didn't seem to be bothered by this was Bob, who had loved being in the water and was excited by all the strange new smells around him, not to mention the sound of little animals moving nearby. Melisande had to work to keep him from romping off into any of the patches of sharp red flowers, which would have sliced his bare feet to ribbons.

The darkening purple sky arched above us, and the air smelled clean and spicy. I think that smell may have been the most alien thing of all. More than the purple sky or the weird flowers or the broccoli-like grass, it forced me to remember that I was a long way from home.

I wondered what time it was on Earth. The Wentar had said that time operates differently on different worlds. Was it possible only a few minutes had passed back home? Or—and this would be much worse—would we get home to find that days, or even years, had gone by?

We had been so busy trying to survive that I hadn't really thought about these things. Now I couldn't get them out of my mind. Was Gramma Walker still sleeping soundly in our house? Or had she woken to find us gone? I had this horrible vision of her in a state of panic, calling our parents to come home from their florists conference, filled with guilt and fear. . . .

"We'd better hurry," I said

Gaspar nodded. "A great deal depends on us. Heavy, heavy is the burden we carry."

"Look, boss," said Albert. "I hate to bring this up, but if we're going to separate, we need to figure out who's going where."

Melisande's snakes began to hiss and writhe. I knew how they felt. Suddenly, splitting up seemed like a terrible idea.

"Clearly, I must make the trip to Flinduvia," said the Wentar. "However, I think it would be a good idea if one of you Morleys came along. Assuming I actually locate Martin, it may be reassuring for him if a member of his family is with me."

"Perhaps I should go," said Gaspar. "He is my twin, after all."

The Wentar shook his head. "Aside from me, you're the only one who has the knowledge and training to lead a trip to the Land of the Dead, Gaspar. Therefore, you must go back to Earth with Sarah and Anthony."

"I vill go to Flinduvia," said Ludmilla.

"I'll go, too," said Albert instantly.

Sarah nudged me. "I think he likes her," she whispered.

I looked at Ludmilla. Aside from the fangs, she was definitely a babe. Even so, the idea that Albert had a crush on her was pretty weird.

"If Ludmilla issss going to Flinduvia, then I sssshould accompany Gaspar and the children," said Melisande. She paused, then added, "It issss probably besssst we bring Bob with our group. He'll be lessss trouble that way."

Bob licked her face.

"Oh, sssstop," she said, pushing him away.

We walked for a time in silence. It was clear the Morleys were upset about the idea of separating.

"What about those Flinduvians who were chasing us?" asked Sarah suddenly. "Are you sure they didn't come through after us?"

"I told you, you cannot track someone through a Starry Door," said the Wentar calmly.

"Well, then, won't they still be waiting for us back at Morley Manor?" she asked.

It was exactly the sort of sensible thing I could count on her to think of.

"That, too, is unlikely," said the Wentar. "Patience is not one of their virtues, and I expect they will have left by now, especially as they have no idea when, or even if, we would return. However, your concerns are not entirely unjustified."

"There's always room for despair when you're around," muttered Albert.

The Wentar ignored him. Turning to Gaspar, he said, "In the odd event that they *are* still there, you can use this sonic disruptor to buy yourself some time. Just fling it to the floor. It will create an effective . . . distraction." As he spoke, he pressed a silvery disk, about three inches across and an inch thick, into Gaspar's hand.

The lizard-headed scientist slid the disk into the pocket of his lab coat. Then he and the Wentar got into a conversation about how, exactly, we were going to get to the Land of the Dead. I listened eagerly but other than the fact that Morley Manor seemed to be the best starting place, I couldn't make much sense of it.

It wasn't long before we reached the place where we had stepped out of the Starry Door.

It wasn't there!

"What happened to it?" I cried, afraid we were going to be stuck on this frogworld forever.

"Doors such as this are not constantly open," said Gaspar gently. "Think of the trouble it would cause if they were! Not only would people be hopping from planet to planet all the time, which would be bad enough, but all sorts of wildlife might wander through as well. That would really create chaos!"

Melisande began to laugh, and her snakes made a kind of choked hissing that I realized must be their version of a giggle.

"What's so funny?" asked Sarah.

"I wassss thinking of what people on Earth would ssssay if they could ssssee the petssss I keep on Zzzzentarazzzzna."

"What *is* Zentarazna?" I asked.

"It issss the plasssse we would rather be," she answered. That was all she would say about it, even though Sarah pestered her with questions while we waited for Gaspar and the Wentar to reopen the Starry Door—a process that involved a lot of singing and hand waving as far as I could tell.

Suddenly I felt a change in the air around us. We stopped talking and looked toward where Gaspar and the Wentar were working.

"Look!" whispered Sarah.

It was awesome. First there was nothing but air in front of us. Then, slowly, a shimmering oval began to appear. In the center of that oval was the Starry Door.

It seemed as if it took forever for the door to finish taking shape, though really it was only about ten minutes. The thing is, once it *was* ready, I sort of wished it wasn't. Even though I was eager to get back to Earth, I was terrified of what we had to do once we got there.

The purple sky was nearly dark above us now, the first stars just starting to appear. Some small creatures began singing in the grass. Our group stood without moving, and I realized for the first time that once we split up it was possible we might never see the others again. Both groups were going on dangerous missions—missions from which they might never return. It was clear this was much on the mind of the Family Morleskievich as well. Finally Gaspar stepped forward and said to Ludmilla, "Be careful, little sister."

They hugged each other for a long time.

I looked at my own little sister. Even though she's an incredible pain and bugs the daylights out of me, I realized that I would do just about anything to keep someone else from hurting her. I realized something else, too: As horrible as the monsters of Morley Manor looked, their feelings were, in many ways, not that different from ours.

The rest of us said our good-byes. The Wentar grasped me firmly by the hand. It was the first time I had touched him, and his skin had a kind of papery feel. Yet there was also a tingle of power and energy in it. "You have been brave, Anthony," he said. "But there are greater challenges to come. Much depends on you and your sister. Do not lose courage, and do not forget the power and strength that come from the ties of love that bind a family together."

Albert took me by the hand, too. His hand was more leathery, and the back of it was covered with thick hair. "Thank you for thawing us out," he said.

"It was an honor," I replied.

Then it was time to go. The Wentar stepped to the Starry Door and pulled it open. As before, it revealed the black void sprinkled with stars. Bending, the Wentar touched one in the lower right corner. "I want to go *there*," he said.

The door rippled. The Wentar stepped forward, Ludmilla and Albert at his side.

An instant later, they were gone.

Then it was our turn.

Standing in front of the door, Gaspar squared his shoulders, muttered something that might have been a prayer, pointed at one of the stars, and said, "I want to go *there*!"

The door rippled.

Hoping that Gaspar had pointed to the star that would take us back to Morley Manor, Sarah and I followed him through the door, Melisande and Bob close behind us.

MY BODY WAS still tingling when I realized we were back in the upstairs hallway of Morley Manor—or, to be more precise, the strange hallway that stretched *beyond* Morley Manor.

"No matter how far one wanders, there's still no place like home," said Gaspar. His voice was dry, and I couldn't tell if he was joking or not.

He started toward the secret entrance that led

back into the house. We came to the shreds of the black wall that had been sliced open by the Flinduvians. Though the air was still, the tatters moved and shifted, as if blown by a wind from another world. Gaspar gathered a handful and looked at them sadly. "Such power," he whispered. "Such anger."

I assumed he was talking about the Flinduvians.

He held the tatters aside so the rest of us could pass.

"What time issss it, do you ssssupposssse?" hissed Melisande, once we were on the other side of the bookcase, back in the real Morley Manor.

None of us was wearing a watch. Despite the weird chiming we had heard when we came in, there were no clocks in the house; they had been sold with the rest of the furniture. From where we were standing, we couldn't even tell if it was light or dark outside.

"Come," said Gaspar. "If we go outdoors we can get a sense of the time—though that won't tell us what *day* it is."

"I hope we haven't been gone too long," said Sarah nervously. She slipped her hand into mine as we walked down the stairs. I kept looking over my shoulder, wondering if the Flinduvians were waiting to leap out and ambush us. But there was no sign of them, other than some holes smashed in the walls.

We stepped outside. Bob leaped over the railing and began running around, sniffing at bushes. Gaspar simply walked to the edge of the porch and began scanning the sky. I went to stand beside him. It was still dark, but a hint of gray was pearling up in the east.

"I'd say it's about four in the morning," he muttered at last. "That makes things a little tricky, since we need to wait until midnight to make the crossing to the Land of the Dead."

"We sssstill don't know what day it issss," pointed out Melisande.

"There's a paper box two blocks up," said Sarah. "We can check the date there."

Gaspar glanced around. "I am not comfortable going that far from the house. I would rather not be seen."

I had gotten so used to the monsters that I hadn't thought about that. When we had carried them to Morley Manor, they had been about five inches high, so it had been no problem to hide them. But at full size, Gaspar was well over six feet—not to mention his having a lizardy head that was at least two feet long. He was not the kind of guy you saw walking down the street every day in a place like Owl's Roost.

"I'll check the paper," said Sarah. "Be right back."

"I'll go with you," I said quickly.

"Wait!" said Gaspar.

It was too late. Sarah and I had bounded off the porch and were almost at the gate.

I think Gaspar was afraid we might run off on him, but the reason I had followed Sarah was much simpler: I was still worried about the Flinduvians, and I didn't want her bumping into them on her own. What good I could have done by being with her I couldn't tell you, so in some ways it was a stupid thing to do. But in my heart, it felt right. Even though we annoy each other, we had been sticking closer together since Grampa Walker died.

"Uh-oh," I said when I got a look at the paper in the box. "Gramma must be going crazy! We've been gone a whole day!"

Sarah looked at the newspaper for a moment, then began to laugh. "No we haven't, Anthony. It was only a night."

"But that's the Monday paper. And it was Sunday when we went into Morley Manor."

"And after Sunday midnight it was Monday morning," said Sarah, as if she were explaining something to an idiot.

"Yeah, but it's just barely morning. The paper wouldn't be out yet. So it must have been here since yesterday. Which means this must be Tuesday."

"Uh-uh," said Sarah, shaking her head. "This is the *morning* paper. They start putting them out at about four or so. Besides, the box is still full. If this was yesterday's paper, there would be hardly any left. So it must be *Monday* morning. If we get home before Gramma wakes up, she'll never know we were gone."

"All right, let's go back and tell Gaspar the good news," I said, feeling kind of grumpy. How did she know all this stuff, anyway?

GASPAR AND MELISANDE were standing on the walk just inside the gate, out of sight from anyone who might happen by—though passersby were pretty unlikely, considering the time and the location. Their worried expressions changed to relief when they saw us returning.

"Everything is fine," I said. "It's Monday morning, just like it should be, and . . . yikes! I forgot!"

13

The Original Package

"WHAT?" CRIED MELISANDE and Gaspar together. "What is it?"

"Monday," I said, my voice weak. "That's when they're going to tear down Morley Manor. They'll be starting in just a few hours!"

"O perfidious world!" cried Gaspar indignantly. "That a man's home should be subject to such whims of fortune!"

Melisande's snakes began to writhe furiously.

Bob crouched at her side, whining piteously.

"I told you they were going to do it," I pointed out.

Of course, that had been more than five hours ago. A lot had happened to us since then, including being chased by horrible aliens, making a trip to another planet, and finding out that the very souls of Earth's dead were in danger.

"We must take quick action," said Gaspar. "No time for thought, no chance for sweet contemplation. Such is the darkness of the world." He looked from side to side, almost as if hoping to find someone to help him. His shoulders slumped. We were on our own.

"All right," he said. "Anthony, Sarah—please come back inside with us. We will need your help in returning to our human shapes."

"You want ussss to turn back?" cried Melisande in alarm. "Here? On *Earth*?"

It was clear she didn't like the idea. Judging by the horrible hissing and fizzing they set up, her snakes liked it even less.

"We have no choice," said Gaspar. He sounded apologetic.

"You can turn back into humans whenever you want?" I asked, startled by the idea.

"What is a human?" asked Gaspar, spreading his hands. "Is it form or face that gives us sweet humanity, or is it something deeper and more real?"

"Jusssst anssssswer the quessssstion," hissed Melisande impatiently.

Gaspar sighed. "Yes, we can turn back, but not easily. At least, it's not easy here. In fact, the process is quite painful—which is probably a metaphor, though I haven't yet figured out for what."

"Do you mind telling us how you got this way?" asked Sarah.

"Not at all, when we have time. At the moment we've got work to do."

"What about Bob?" I asked, gesturing toward the werehuman cocker spaniel.

"There's nothing we can do about him right now," said Gaspar. "His transformation was of a different sort than ours. Now, follow me."

He led the way back upstairs to his laboratory. For a moment I was worried that the Flinduvians might have smashed it in a fit of spite, so I was relieved to see that it was still intact.

The green jewel called The Heart of Zentarazna that provided power for the whole operation still rested in the control box.

Even our yellow raincoats were right where we had left them.

"Now listen carefully," said Gaspar. "I'm going to show you how to operate the equipment. But there is something else, something more important. This is not going to be pleasant for Melisande and me. We will plead for you to stop the process. *You must not do this!* No matter how we beg or scream, no matter what we say, you must not stop the transformation. To do so would be catastrophic. Is that clear?"

"Clear," I said, feeling uneasy.

Gaspar talked us through the order in which we had to push the buttons and pull the levers. He did it twice, then made me repeat it to him two more times. When he was satisfied, he took Melisande by the hand and they went to stand beneath the same glass chambers we had used to enlarge them.

Even after they were in place, I waited for Gaspar's nod before pulling the lever that would lower the tubes. As the chambers descended from the ceiling Melisande's snakes started thrashing wildly, tying themselves in knots.

We heard the dull thunk of the glass against the platform. A moment later Gaspar nodded again. Instantly Sarah and I set to work, pulling levers and shifting dials. Soon a fantastic humming filled the room, getting gradually louder and louder. Sparks crackled through the glass chambers, which began to fill with green mist. Electricity—or maybe some other kind of power I don't know about—skittered over the surface of the cylinders.

All at once Gaspar began to scream.

"We've got to turn it off!" cried Sarah in alarm.

"No!" I said fiercely. "He told us this would happen."

Gaspar screamed again and began pounding on the side of the tube. Melisande uttered a high-pitched shriek that seemed to wind around his, spiraling upward.

I felt as if someone was scraping shards of glass down a blackboard.

Melisande was on her knees now. I could see her snakes through the green mist, thrashing, thrashing, stretching out to new lengths as if they were trying to separate from her head.

"Stop it!" sobbed Sarah. "Stop it, Anthony! You have to stop it!"

"We can't!" I said, though there was nothing in the world I wanted more at that moment than to do just that. "If we stop now, Gaspar and Melisande might be caught halfway between human and monster forever!"

Gaspar screamed a third time. "For the love of God, Anthony, stop the process! I was wrong, I was wrong. Stop it if you have a shred of mercy in your soul!"

He beat his head against the clear wall of the cylinder, sobbing piteously.

"I can't stand it!" cried Sarah. "Turn it off, Anthony!"

She lunged for the main lever. I caught her just in time. She may be nicer than I am, but sometimes nice isn't the answer. I held on to her with all my might as she fought to get to the controls. It wasn't easy, because I couldn't stand the screams either and wanted desperately for them to end. Even worse, I was secretly afraid that something really had gone wrong, that Gaspar and Melisande were being tortured, maybe even dying. But Gaspar had been deadly serious in his instructions: *I must not stop the process once it had started.*

Sarah broke free of my grasp. I tackled her and we both fell to the floor.

The screams of Gaspar and Melisande were louder and more desperate than ever.

I felt as if I was being tortured myself. Was I doing the right thing? I was on the verge of letting Sarah go, of letting her pull the lever that would halt the horrible process, when I heard three loud snaps, just as Gaspar had said we would.

Instantly the mist in the chambers turned purple.

"There!" I said, letting go of Sarah. "Now we can turn it off."

Her face was streaked with tears. "I hate you!" she sobbed.

Ignoring her, I stood up and pulled the lever that raised the chambers.

Coughing and choking, Gaspar and Melisande stepped out.

Bob took one look at the two of them and began to howl.

"Holy mackerel!" cried Sarah, wiping at her tears with the back of her hand. "You guys look like movie stars!" Turning toward me, she muttered, "Sorry about the fuss, Anthony."

"Don't worry about it, kid," I replied softly. "When you're big like me, you'll know better."

"You're a booger," she said. She probably would have said more, but she was too interested in Gaspar and Melisande.

The human Gaspar had jet-black hair; a strong, prominent nose; a high forehead; and wide-set brown eyes. He stretched and rubbed his arms, then shook his head like a dog that had just climbed out of the water.

Melisande, still wearing her slinky dress, reached up to touch her own hair. She made a terrible face. "How boring!" she muttered, as she ran her hands through the tangled mass of glossy raven curls. It was strange to hear her speak with no hissing.

"So—now what do we do?" I asked.

"First Gaspar and I have to change our clothes," said Melisande decisively.

I thought this was a terrible idea. Her dress looked spectacular. But she was right—she couldn't walk around Owl's Roost that way without attracting attention.

Actually, she probably couldn't walk around any-where that way without attracting attention.

"Melisande speaks truth," said Gaspar. "Too often a man is judged on how he dresses. I must work fast this morning and will need every advantage I can get. Fond as I am of this lab coat, it has seen better days."

"Changing your clothes is a good idea, but I don't think there's much chance of doing it," said Sarah.

"Why not?" asked Melisande.

"Well, aside from the fact that any clothes you had would be fifty-some years out of style, I doubt there are any here. Remember, they had a sale to clear the place out before the wreckers came. That's how Anthony got you to begin with."

"Can you help us?" asked Gaspar desperately. "I must get to a lawyer immediately. They may be a vile species and the curse of humanity, but they're our only hope at the moment."

Sarah glanced at me. "Do you suppose they could wear Mom and Dad's clothes?"

I didn't think Mom and Dad would be particularly pleased by the idea. On the other hand, we were in so far at this point that I figured a little thing like loaning our parents' clothes to a couple of recently transformed monsters shouldn't slow us down. "Hard to say. I think Gaspar is a little taller than Dad. And Melisande is a little more . . ." I let the sentence drop. "I don't know. It might work."

"Let's go," said Gaspar.

"What about Bob?" asked Sarah.

Gaspar looked at Bob. The werehuman began to whine.

"We'd better take him with us," said Gaspar. "If anyone comes along, we'll just have to hide him. Do you think you can keep him quiet, Melisande?"

She looked at Bob, then shrugged. "It won't be easy, but I think I can manage it."

As it turned out, hiding Bob wasn't necessary. When we went outside a pale light was creeping across the sky. Bob began to bark. Then he flopped onto his side and kicked, the way dogs do when they're dreaming. Then he rolled over and over.

In a few moments, he wriggled out of his clothes, a floppy-eared cocker spaniel, panting and wagging his tail.

"That is too weird," said Sarah, as Bob came trotting over to lick her hand.

"What a good dog!" cried Melisande, patting Bob's head.

"Come along," said Gaspar. "We have to hurry."

Easy for him to say. He wasn't going to have to explain all this to his grandmother.

We slipped into the house. Gramma was still asleep, though how long that would last, I wasn't certain. Given her deafness, we weren't likely to wake her with our noise. On the other hand, she was an early riser. The one I was really worried about was Mr. Perkins. But when he came loping into the kitchen and bared his nasty little monkey fangs at us, Melisande said sharply, "Oh, don't be silly! Settle down and be a nice boy."

To my astonishment, Mr. Perkins did exactly that. He trotted docilely to her side, and when she reached down her arm, he climbed up and sat gently on her shoulder.

"Melisande has always had a way with animals," said Gaspar. I could hear a kind of pride in his voice at his younger sister's talent.

I shook my head. We had seen a lot of bizarre things that night, but the sight of the fabulously beautiful Melisande in her skintight, slinky dress, with Mr. Perkins on her shoulder, running his paws delicately through her curly black hair, was as weird as any of them.

Sarah yawned, which got me started, too. "I don't think I've ever been so tired in my entire life," I muttered.

"Please," said Gaspar urgently. "Just help us find something to wear. Then you can sleep."

Sarah led the way to our parents' bedroom, where Gramma was sleeping. Even though I didn't think she would hear us, we moved quietly.

It took about a half an hour, and a few safety

pins, but we finally got Gaspar and Melisande looking pretty acceptable. Dad's suit looked sort of doofy
on Gaspar, but as Sarah said, he was so handsome he
could get away with it. Melisande didn't look quite as
wonderful as she had in her own dress, but that was
probably just as well.

"Now what?" Sarah asked.

"Now Melisande and I go wake up some poor
lawyer and try to save Morley Manor," said Gaspar.
"It's not going to be easy, but we should at least be
able to stop the wreckers for a day. After all, we are
the rightful heirs. In the meantime, you two get
some rest. I want you fresh and ready for our trip to
the Land of the Dead."

14

Past Meets Present

DESPITE THE FACT that I was exhausted, my mind was in such a whirl that I didn't know if I would be able to sleep or not. But the minute I hit the sheets, I fell into a sleep so deep it was like being dead.

Good practice for what was to come, I suppose.

I didn't wake up until noon.

When I staggered out to the kitchen, I found Gramma standing at the counter, kneading some bread dough. Mr. Perkins was sitting on his perch, eating an apple. He snarled at me when I came in. Obviously, Melisande's influence had worn off. In fact, the whole scene looked so normal that I began to wonder if everything that I thought had happened the night before had just been some weird dream after all.

Gramma didn't hear me come in, of course. I went and stood next to her, so I wouldn't startle her when she realized I was there.

She jumped a little, anyway. "Good morning, slugabed," she said cheerfully. "What did you two do last night, sneak out and watch TV after I had gone to sleep?"

"Something like that," I said, looking straight at her. This is the best way to talk to Gramma Walker. She uses the way your lips move to help figure out what you're saying. "Is Sarah up?" I added.

"She's in the bathroom. Why don't you pour yourself a bowl of cereal?"

That sounded like a good idea. I had been so tired when we got in that I'd forgotten I was also starving.

Mr. Perkins hissed at me as I went to the cupboard. The sound reminded me of Melisande's snakes. I wondered how she and Gaspar were making out with their quest to find a lawyer to help them save Morley Manor.

Before I could worry about it too much, I heard

the doorbell. Gramma didn't hear it, of course, but when I stood up and started toward the door, she said, "I'll get it, Anthony. You eat."

While she was gone, Sarah came back into the kitchen. I was about to ask her if last night had really happened when Gramma came back, too. She had an odd look on her face. Melisande and Gaspar were behind her, Bob trotting happily at their heels.

"These people say they're friends of yours," said Gramma, looking a little puzzled. (It may seem strange to some of you that she would let them in, but you have to remember that in Owl's Roost, Nebraska, people still leave their doors unlocked at night. We are not what you would call the crime capital of the world.)

"How did you make out?" I asked, jumping to my feet.

Gaspar smiled. "Justice has triumphed! We obtained a temporary restraining order to stop the demolition. Morley Manor still stands!"

"Gracious!" said Gramma. "What do you two have to do with Morley Manor?"

Then she narrowed her eyes. Her hands began to tremble.

"Gaspar?" she whispered.

He looked at her curiously.

She clutched at her heart. "*Gaspar!*" she said again, and this time her voice sounded accusing.

Gaspar looked at her more intently. Suddenly his eyes grew wide. *"Ethel?"* he cried in astonishment.

Gramma staggered and grabbed the back of a chair. Slowly, she lowered herself into it. "Gaspar," she murmured. "Melisande. Bob!"

"What's going on here?" I asked, totally baffled.

"That's what I want to know," said Gramma. She sounded terrified.

Gaspar turned to me. "Your grandmother and I were once engaged to be married," he said, his voice thick with emotion.

"It *is* you," whispered Gramma in awe. "But how is it possible? *Where have you been?*"

"It's a long story," said Gaspar.

"He's not kidding," I said.

"Sit," said Gramma firmly. "Tell."

WE SPENT most of that afternoon at the kitchen table. There were two stories that needed to be told: what had happened to Sarah and me in the past twenty-four hours, and what had happened to Gaspar and the other Morleys over fifty years ago. Sarah, of course, also wanted to know all about Gaspar and Gramma having been engaged. But they seemed hesitant to talk about it, as if the topic was too painful to touch, and after a few questions she gave up.

"I could tell it was upsetting them," she told me later.

As for what had happened to the Morleys . . .

"We don't actually know all of the story our-selves," confessed Gaspar, "and won't, unless the Wentar is able to bring back not only my brother, but the clone that had pretended to be him for all those years. But I can tell you how it began." He folded his hands on the table in front of him. "I was, as you know, both a scientist and a magician."

"It was considered a great scandal by those who figured it out," put in Gramma Walker.

"Yes, and an even greater scandal when big brother here started going out with a woman so much younger than himself," said Melisande. "Such is the way of a small town."

It took me a moment to realize that the "younger" woman she was talking about was Gramma!

"Don't fool yourself, Melisande," said Gramma sharply. "I've lived in the big city. People there gossip just as much as small-town folk. More, probably. It's just that you have to be better known to get gossiped about by the 'right' people. Go on, Gaspar. I'm eager to find out why you broke my heart."

"Breaking your heart was the last thing I ever in-tended," said Gaspar, reaching out to take her hand.

"Can we skip the romance and tell the story?" I asked. I was still trying to get used to the idea of Gramma being younger than Gaspar, since she now looked thirty or forty years older than him. But then, she had kept on living for the fifty years that the Morleys had been frozen.

Gaspar nodded, his face no longer that of a great lizard, but that of a lean, handsome man. I wondered if Grampa Walker had known about this—which got me to wondering what it would have been like if things had worked out differently and Gaspar actually had married my grandmother.

It was too weird to wrap my mind around.

"Our real troubles started when I discovered the secret of the Starry Doors," he said. "I was angry, because I realized Martin had known it for some time, and had not shared it with me."

"Of course, that was when we still thought Martin was our real brother," said Melisande.

Gaspar sighed. "It changes so much to know the truth. And we haven't had time to think through all that it means. Anyway, since Martin had not told me what he was doing, I returned the favor and did not tell him what *we* were up to. But with Ludmilla, Melisande, Albert, and Bob at my side, I began to explore other worlds. One planet in particular, Zentarazna, held a great fascination for us. In that place, people had learned to shape their own bodies as they wished, to change them as it suited their fancy. Since Melisande and Ludmilla had grown tired of all the attention they got for their great beauty, they quickly embraced the idea of taking on a strange image."

"We tried several," said Melisande. "It was fun. Like changing clothes in a dressing room. And not nearly as difficult to do as it is here," she added, turning to me and Sarah.

Gramma shot her a glance, and I got the sense that they had not liked each other all those years ago.

"Of course," said Gaspar, "Albert was always Albert, and Bob's were-problems had started back in Transylvania. They are who they are. It was Ludmilla, Melisande, and I who played at shape-shifting. In late October of 1948, there was a townwide Halloween party—"

"The last night I ever saw you," murmured Gramma.

Gaspar nodded. "The three of us had decided to go in our altered shapes, which seemed like the best of all possible costumes. Alas, that was the night Martin discovered what we had been doing. A great argument broke out when we got home. Martin pulled out a strange weapon, something I had never seen before. And that's the last thing I remember until I found myself standing on the edge of your bathroom sink, looking up at Anthony and Sarah!"

Gramma squeezed his hand. "I cried for a long time after you disappeared," she whispered.

Gaspar shook his handsome head. "I did not expect this, Ethel. My heart has gone into hiding, and I have no words for what I feel."

I was startled to see tears in his eyes. Then I realized that even though fifty years had gone by for Gramma, for Gaspar it was as if he had last seen her only the day before, seen her young and beautiful, seen her as the woman he was going to marry.

And now she was old.

"There was a great scandal," said Gramma softly. "People suspected that Martin had killed you all. But there were no bodies, so the police couldn't put together a case." She shook her head. "And all that time you were trapped in a box inside Morley Manor. Oh, that Martin! I could just—"

She stopped, unable to finish the sentence, though I wasn't sure if it was because she couldn't bring herself to say something violent in front of me and Sarah, or because she couldn't think of something bad enough to do to Martin.

"He wasn't the real Martin," said Gaspar softly. "Though whether any of us can ever know our true self is a great question, anyway."

"Those fifty years seemed like only a moment to us," added Melisande. "But the world has changed so! We were only out for a few hours this morning, but it was as if we had gone to another planet. Had we not traveled before, been to Zentarazna and other strange places, I do not think I could have coped with all this."

"And now you need to travel again," murmured Gramma, awe and wonder in her voice. "You need to go to the Land of the Dead to see my poor husband."

Gaspar nodded.

"Well," she said, "I'm going with you."

Gaspar started to protest, but it was pointless. I knew that tone of voice. He had as much of a chance of talking Gramma out of going with us as I had of sprouting wings and flying—though the way things had been going lately, I suppose even that wouldn't have surprised me. As for Gramma, she might have been astonished to see Gaspar, might even have felt the stirrings of an old love. But there was no way she was going to miss a chance to visit Grampa.

SINCE GRAMMA could provide the needed connection for the trip, we had a long argument about whether or not Sarah and I should be allowed to come. Gramma thought it was too dangerous. We pointed out what we had already been through, but that didn't convince her. Even Sarah's pleading, which is usually quite effective, did not change Gramma's mind. It was only when I argued that we would probably be in more danger on our own than we would if we went with them that she relented.

So, at eleven o'clock that night, we returned to Morley Manor.

"There's one thing I don't get," said Sarah, as we approached the house. "If the key to making the trip is our connection to Grampa, then why do we have to come back here to do it?"

"Two reasons," said Gaspar. "First, the aura of magic is stronger here. That was one of the reasons we bought the place to begin with, of course. And our work over the years did a great deal to increase that. Besides, we can go deeper into the Earth here, which makes the journey easier."

"So the Land of the Dead is underground?" asked Sarah.

"Not really. From what the Wentar told me, I don't think you can say it is in this world at all. Even so, going underground brings you closer to a certain kind of truth."

By this time we had reached the house. Melisande shuddered when she saw the bulldozer parked in front of it.

"The feathers of doom did indeed sweep close to our family home today," said Gaspar grimly.

Once we were inside, he led the way down the cellar stairs. He held Sarah's flashlight in one hand, in the other a broomstick to knock aside the cobwebs— which were so thick in some places that they looked like a gray silk wall.

On the far side of the basement was a door that led to another stairway, one that took us even deeper into the Earth.

A stray cobweb brushed across my forehead. The air was cold and damp. Bob began to whine.

"It's all right, boy," murmured Melisande, who was walking beside him.

I counted a hundred and thirteen steps as we descended.

"Where did these stairs come from?" asked Sarah.

"Martin built them, of course," said Gaspar. "At one time we would have done it together."

He sounded bitter, and wistful.

Finally we reached the bottom. The chamber we entered was earthen walled, but had a solid ceiling, supported by thick wooden beams.

Gaspar instructed us to lie down and join hands. The dirt floor was cool and damp, but he said closeness to the Earth was important.

"Leave a space for me here," he said, talking to Gramma and me. We shifted apart, still holding hands for the time being.

"Now close your eyes," Gaspar said, turning off the flashlight.

"Why should we close our eyes?" asked Melisande. "It's dark enough already!"

"It will help you move deeper into yourselves," said Gaspar quietly.

I closed my eyes and listened as he worked. He was muttering to himself, strange words that I couldn't quite make out. Every once in a while I heard him strike a match; I could see the flicker of light, even through my closed lids.

A pungent odor filled the room, a weird mingling of freshness and rot, sharp as vinegar, sweet as cider. My head began to whirl.

"Now think of those who have gone before," Gaspar said. A moment later I felt him separate my hand from Gramma's. He lay down between us, then took my hand in his.

The soil was cool, damp, and firm beneath me. I felt almost as if I were lying in a grave.

I turned my thoughts to Grampa, thought of how much I wanted to see him, to tell him that I loved him.

Suddenly I looked down and saw a long silver cord. With a start, I realized that it stretched back to my own body.

Gramma was floating next to me. Near her, I saw Sarah and Melisande. Gaspar was on the other side of me. Even Bob had made it through, looking as surprised as I have ever seen a cocker spaniel look.

Ahead of us, all around us, was a vast space filled with a kind of milky mist. Floating through it were the figures of people, some of them sharply defined, others soft around the edges, so it was hard to make them out. Their moans and mutters filled the air.

I looked down. All I saw was more mist. I had no idea how far above the ground we were—if there even was any ground, for that matter. But I felt so light I had no fear of falling.

"That way!" said Gramma suddenly, her voice strong and firm.

A murmur of astonishment rose from the shapes floating around us.

We followed her. I wasn't sure how we were moving. We didn't flap our arms or anything. It was more like you thought about where you wanted to go, then just sort of moved in that direction.

Ahead of us floated a spirit.

Even from behind he looked familiar. I felt a thickness in my throat, a lump of emotion I couldn't swallow away.

"Hello, Horace," said Gramma softly. "We've come for a little visit."

15

Family Reunion

WHEN GRAMPA TURNED, when Gramma finally saw his face, she started to cry. They weren't real tears, of course, since we weren't actually in our bodies. Still, you could tell she was crying by the way her mouth trembled and her shoulders shook.

As for Grampa, he looked . . . well, he looked odd. He had a lot of expressions moving across his face, things that looked like surprise, happiness, anger, joy, even fear. The really weird thing was that his face was no longer old, the way it had been the last time I'd seen him. But it wasn't young, either. It was as if all the ages he had ever been, all the faces he had worn through the years, had combined somehow. His wrinkles were gone, but his eyes were old and wise.

He was also transparent. That didn't seem all that odd, since we were, too. But unlike us, he had no silver cord leading back to his body, no thread connecting him to the world of the living.

He stared at us for a long time. "You're not dead," he said at last, his voice worried, puzzled, and relieved all at once.

"Well, of course not, Horace," said Gramma matter-of-factly.

I was surprised that she could hear him, since he had barely spoken above a whisper and she was nearly deaf. Then I realized her deafness was part of her physical body, and we had left those behind when we entered the Land of the Dead.

"What are you doing here?" he asked. "And with the children! You shouldn't have come, Ethel!"

"We had to come, sir," said Gaspar.

Grampa turned toward him. His eyes grew wide. "Gaspar?" he said slowly, and beneath the astonishment I could sense a hint of anger in his voice. "Gaspar Morley? And—can it be?—Melisande!" He said her name with something like a sob. "But you're no older than when . . . but you're not dead, either! How can . . . Ethel, what's going on here? What are you doing here with *them*?"

"It's a long story," said Gaspar.

Grampa gestured to the misty void surrounding us. "If there's one thing I've got, it's time."

"Actually, that may not be entirely true," Gaspar replied. "The reason we dared this journey is to bring word to the dead that they are in danger."

"Dead is dead," said Grampa, sounding scornful.

"Really?" asked Gaspar. "It's true that you are dead to the life you once knew. But though you no longer have your body, your *self* still exists. Now that is in danger as well."

Grampa snorted. "You sound like Reverend van Dyke. But don't worry, Gaspar. There's not much temptation around here. I don't think I'm in danger of any major sins at the moment."

Gaspar's handsome face darkened with a scowl of frustration. "The danger is from outside, you old—" He cut himself off and took a deep breath. Then he closed his eyes. I had a feeling he was counting to ten. Maybe higher. Finally he spoke again, sounding somewhat stiff and formal.

"There exists a great and powerful alien race, a group without pity or mercy. These people, the Flinduvians, have found a way to use the souls of

Earth's dead to power a weapon they have created. If they should take you, sir, the result would be a second death. A permanent one. A death not of the body, but of the soul itself. Or perhaps not. We don't really know what happens when a soul is used in this weapon of theirs. It could be far worse than mere oblivion."

Now Grampa did look frightened. "You're joking," he whispered.

"I did not travel all the way to the Land of the Dead for the sake of a prank," said Gaspar sharply. "Now, is there someone you can take us to, a leader of any sort here?"

"I never thought I'd hear someone say 'take me to your leader' to a *ghost*," whispered Sarah.

"I never thought I'd make a trip to the Land of the Dead," I replied softly.

Grampa's face twisted into a familiar scowl. I recognized it as his thinking look. "I don't believe there's really a leader in this place," he said. "But I haven't been here all that long, so maybe there's something or someone I don't know about. Some souls greeted me when I arrived, helped calm me, kept me from being afraid. But since then I've been pretty much on my own."

"What have you been doing, Grampa?" Sarah asked.

"Waiting. Thinking. Trying to let go." He glanced at my grandmother. "It's hard, Ethel. I don't *want* to let go."

"Let go of what?" asked Sarah. We had both floated close to him, and now she reached out to take his hand. She couldn't really touch him, of course. Touch is for the living.

"Of the world," he said slowly. "Of life." He turned to look at Gramma. "Mostly I didn't want to let go of you, my dear. But that's what I'm supposed to do, I guess. I'm not really supposed to be here. None of us is. We're supposed to move on to . . . Well, I don't know exactly what. To something else. But I couldn't stop thinking about our life together." He looked at Gaspar again, then added bitterly, "I didn't expect you to show up here with my old rival."

Gramma smiled. "Are you jealous, you old fool?" she asked, in her most loving voice.

"Jealous of the living," said Grampa.

Gramma stretched her hand toward him, but she couldn't touch him, any more than Sarah could. "I suspect that very jealousy would keep you here, if nothing else did, my love. You've got to let go, Horace. But not yet. Not until this nightmare is over." She turned to me and said softly, "This is a nightmare, isn't it, Anthony? I mean, I am only dreaming, right?"

I longed to be able to tell her that was the case.

But Gramma was fierce about the truth and didn't like even the tiniest lies. Besides, who knew what else we were going to have to deal with before this was all over? If she thought this was a dream, it might lull her, make her less sharp, less ready to act. And that was a luxury we couldn't afford.

So I shook my head. "It's no dream, Gramma."

She sighed. "Oh, I knew that. I was just sort of hoping . . . Well, never mind. What do we do now, Gaspar?"

Gaspar looked uncertain, which was unusual for him. "I guess we try to deliver our warning. After that we go back to the world of the living, to see if the others have returned from Flinduvia."

Gramma turned back to Grampa. "Well, there it is, Horace. You have to help us deliver our warning. I can't take the children home until we do."

She held out her arms and floated toward him.

Gaspar gestured to the rest of our group, and we turned to give the two old people, one living and one dead, a few minutes to themselves.

I used the time while Gramma and Grampa were whispering to each other to get a better look at the place we were in.

There wasn't much to see, or so I thought at first. It was gray and misty, and seemed to roll on forever. Though it didn't have anything you could call land-scape or scenery, I did get a sense of up and down, which was sort of weird. But we were all floating the same way up, as were the occasional dead people who drifted past. So I figured my sense of up and down was genuine.

The ghosts—I guess that's what you would call them—pretty much ignored us. That was fine as far as I was concerned. The only time they looked our way was when Bob growled at them.

I figure they weren't used to seeing cocker spaniels in the Land of the Dead.

"Shush," whispered Melisande. "You're disturbing them."

Bob whimpered, and floated against her side.

"I don't like it here," whispered Sarah, who was floating almost as close to my side as Bob was to Melisande's. "It feels cold."

Gaspar nodded. "It is not pleasant. But remember, this is not where you will spend eternity. This is a place for those who have not yet moved on."

It's HARD TO HAVE a sense of time in the Land of the Dead, so I don't really know how long it was before Gaspar made a noise in his throat to interrupt my grandparents.

Grampa looked startled, as if he had forgotten the rest of us were there.

His voice unusually gentle, Gaspar said, "What would you suggest we do next, Horace?"

Grampa looked at Gaspar for a long time. "I don't know," he said at last.

"Is there no one to contact?"

"Not that I can think of."

They went back and forth like that a couple more times until I finally got sick of it. I don't know what came over me. I had just had enough, I guess. Anyway, I threw my head back and yelled, "Helllllp! We need to talk to someone! Who's in charge here, anyway?"

The silence that followed my outburst was broken when Melisande started to laugh.

It was a rich, beautiful sound.

And it was like bait.

16

Ivanoma

As THE SOUND of Melisande's laugh tinkled and chimed through the mist, I saw the ghosts around us stop their slow drifting. They turned and began to move toward us. Within moments, we were surrounded by dozens of translucent men and women (and a few children), all staring at Melisande with a look I can only describe as *hunger*.

"Laughter is something you don't hear much of in these parts," explained Grampa softly.

Melisande looked nervous, but I figured this was our big chance. "Listen, everyone," I said, "we've got a problem. Is there anyone in this place we can talk to—anyone who's sort of in charge?"

The dead people glanced at one another. Finally a sad-eyed woman in an old-fashioned dress said, "No one is in charge here. But perhaps you could talk to Ivanoma."

"Who's that?" I asked. I was a little surprised that the grown-ups were letting me carry the conversation, but I guess they figured I had started it and unless I made some mistake they'd let me keep it going.

"Ivanoma is a . . . Well, it's sort of a counselor," said the woman.

"*It?*" I asked.

"Ivanoma is too—" The dead woman paused, then said slowly, "Well, it's too *much* to be a mere he or she."

The others murmured in agreement.

"Don't look at me," said Grampa, when we all turned in his direction. "I've never heard of this Ivanoma, whatever it is."

"How do we find our way to this muchness of a being?" asked Gaspar.

The woman looked at our silver cords, then said hesitantly, "I'm not sure you should go that far."

That made me nervous. If there was one thing I didn't want to do, it was break the connection that held me to my body.

"The cords will hold," said Gaspar confidently.

Melisande leaned over. "I hope Brother knows what he's talking about," she whispered in my ear.

I looked at her in horror. But before I could say anything, the woman who had mentioned Ivanoma said, "Follow me."

TO TRAVEL IN the Land of the Dead is strange. At first I thought there was little to mark the passing of distance, because everything looks the same. But as we moved on, I began to see vague hints of the world of the living. They were little more than shapes in the mist, different shades and tones in the gray, like the images you sometimes get when your TV isn't tuned in well. The difference now was that it was all very real. I realized we were moving *very* fast. I began to worry even more about the silver cords. How far could they stretch?

Suddenly we plunged downward.

Below us stretched a great lake of ice. Chained flat on its back in the center of the lake was the most beautiful creature I had ever seen. It was shaped like a human, but it was enormous, maybe a hundred feet long. Vast, perfectly formed wings stretched from its shoulders across the clear ice. Its face was calm and noble, with a broad, high brow and a mouth that seemed to be just on the verge of a frown on one side, just on the verge of a smile on the other. The sight of it made my heart ache with a longing to coax that smile into bloom.

The being—I assumed it was Ivanoma—lay very still, staring upward into the mist and the darkness. Clusters of the dead surrounded it, leaning against its sides, floating around its huge and magnificent head, resting on its breast.

From its beautiful eyes flowed a never-ending stream of tears.

Some of the dead were bathing in them.

I felt fear, and awe, and pity, as we sank toward the creature.

Suddenly Ivanoma blinked and lifted its head. Then it raised one vast and shapely arm. As it did, the chains that held it to the ice separated as if they were made of nothing but mist—though they had looked as solid as steel just a moment earlier.

"Why have the living come to the Land of the Dead?" it asked in a whisper that had as many tones, as much music, as a choir.

As it spoke, it held out its hand in a clear invitation for us to land upon it.

So we did. Though our bodies were not really there—though we were, in truth, lighter than air—I could see the great being flinch when we touched it. The palm of its hand sank as if a great weight had just been dropped into it.

We stood in the center of Ivanoma's hand and it lowered us, to hold us right before its eyes.

Its eyes.

If I had a hundred years, I couldn't tell you what it meant to look into those eyes, except to say that it was like drowning in pain and beauty, and I was afraid I might never be able to look at the regular world, at anything else, again.

My mother told me once that the memory of pain fades. She said if it didn't, women would never have more than one baby.

I think that must be true for other things as well, things like beauty, and love. If the memory of gazing into those eyes—each of which was a yard wide and several thousand miles deep—had not faded, I doubt I could move in the world today. I would only sit and remember.

For a long time none of us spoke. Finally it was Sarah, the question machine, who asked, "Are you Ivanoma?"

The vast being nodded.

"Are you an angel?" I asked.

It nodded again.

"Why are you here? Why are you so sad?"

None of this was what we had come to say. But it was all that I could think of.

"I made a mistake once," whispered the angel in a voice that would have made Mozart weep with envy because he could never write music that beautiful. "I chose the wrong side in an ancient war. I am paying for my sin."

"But your chains don't hold you," I said, thinking of how it had lifted its hand to receive us.

Ivanoma actually smiled, and I thought that I would die of joy on the spot.

"My chains are of my own making, and I can break them at any time. I *choose* to be here, to console the dead, to offer them help, and guidance, and love, when they are ready to receive it."

I saw Gramma nudge Grampa, as if to say, "You should have taken advantage of this, you old fool."

"The dead need your help now," I said.

Ivanoma raised a single eyebrow. The gesture was like a sunrise.

Quickly, I told the angel what we knew about the Flinduvians.

Its frown nearly killed me.

"I know this to be true," it whispered in a voice that throbbed with pain, as if it held the weight of ten thousand years of human misery. "I have sensed five times in the last moments—you must understand, moments are different to me than they are to you—I have sensed five times someone being wrenched from the Land of the Dead, heard a cry of terror, felt a stab of fear different from the fear I feel when they enter here. I did not know what it meant."

"Can you help?" I cried.

"I can warn the dead," Ivanoma replied.

"Surely you can do more than that," I said urgently. "You are so strong, so powerful."

"I am bound," replied Ivanoma.

"But you can break the chains!"

"I have promised not to."

And that was all it would say. It was all we had come for, really. We wanted to warn the dead. Ivanoma said it would do that for us. Our mission was accomplished. But still . . .

"Come," whispered Gaspar. "It's time for us to leave."

He might as well have said it was time to rip my heart out of my chest and drop it, still beating, into the dog's dish.

"Leave?" I cried. "We can't leave!"

"You must," whispered Ivanoma. "The living do not belong here. It was brave of you to come, but you must go back where you belong. Let me warn the dead. You tend to the living."

The angel closed its eyes and laid its head back against the frozen lake.

It was like being released from a trap you didn't know was holding you. I could never have left the Land of the Dead as long as I was looking into those eyes. Now I was free to go.

And we did go, almost instantly, for in the space

of less than a heartbeat we were back in our bodies, back in the world of the living.

It was clear that Ivanoma had hurried us on our way.

It was also soon clear that the angel had made another mistake.

17

Grampa

WHEN I OPENED my eyes, I saw nothing but deep blackness. For a minute I feared we hadn't made it back after all. Then I remembered we had left our bodies in a sub-sub-sub-basement of Morley Manor, and that the place was completely dark.

I heard Sarah stirring beside me. "Anthony?" she whispered. "Are you there?"

"I'm here," I said quietly.

"Did all that really happen?"

"I think so."

"It was real," said Gaspar. I heard him fumbling around. He struck a match. Even though it was a tiny flame, in the darkness its sudden flare seemed horribly bright. As I blinked against it I saw that Melisande was sitting up, brushing herself off. Bob was still lying on his side, twitching and whining.

Gramma was not moving at all.

I scrambled to my feet to see if she was okay. As I did, I heard a familiar voice cry, *Ethel! Ethel, are you all right?*

I stopped dead, so to speak.

"Grampa?" I said softly. "Grampa, is that you?"

Uh-huh. He sounded subdued, embarrassed almost.

"Where are you?"

I heard Gaspar curse as the match's flame reached his fingertips. He dropped it. We were in darkness again.

"Anthony, who are you talking to?" asked Sarah.

Gramma groaned.

Thank goodness she's alive! said Grampa.

"Where are you?" I shouted.

"Right here," said Sarah.

"Not you," I snapped. "Grampa!"

I'm right here, too, said Grampa.

Suddenly I realized what he meant. Horrified, I grabbed the sides of my head and shouted, "What are you doing in there?"

He sighed. *I'm sorry, Anthony. Whatever Ivanoma did when it sent you all back made it possible for me to—well, to sort of hitch a ride with you. I landed in your body.*

"You *what?*"

Grampa sighed. *I didn't mean to do it. I'm not even sure how it happened, except that I've missed your grandmother so much. I think maybe having been so close to her, having seen her again, I just couldn't let her go. So I . . . came along for the ride.*

"But this is—"

I was interrupted by someone shaking me. "Anthony!" said Gaspar sharply. "Are you all right?"

He had found the flashlight. A dim yellow glow filled the cellar. Suddenly I realized that though I had been talking to Grampa out loud, his answers had all been inside my head.

I must have sounded as if I had lost my mind.

Don't tell them I'm here! said Grampa urgently.

"What?"

Your grandmother won't like it. She'll be mad. Please, Anthony—I'll leave as soon as I can.

I didn't say anything for a minute.

PLEASE!

I sighed. Grampa had always been good to me. What was I going to do? Tattle on him? Send him back to the Land of the Dead?

We'll talk about this later, I thought, hoping he would understand me if I spoke only in my head.

Thanks, Anthony. You're a good boy.

Well, obviously he could understand my thoughts. Out loud I said, "Sorry, Gaspar. Guess I was woozy from the trip."

"Speak up, Anthony," said a voice from below me.

"Gramma!" I cried. "You're all right!"

"Well, mostly," she said. "My hearing is gone again. Too bad about that. No surprise, though."

She started to stand up. *Help her!* said Grampa, but Gaspar beat me to it. I could sense Grampa's annoyance. *He was always after her,* he muttered.

I doubted that Gaspar was still interested in Gramma now that she was more than fifty years older than she had been when he last saw her. Then I wondered if Grampa had picked up on that thought. He didn't mention it if he had.

"Well," said Gramma, once she was on her feet again. "I must say I never expected anything like this when I told your parents I would watch you children for the weekend."

Her voice was kind of shaky, for which I couldn't blame her.

"We'd better get upstairs," said Gaspar. He sounded a little shaky, too, which made me nervous, since he was the closest thing we had to a leader. "I wonder when the others will get back?"

What he didn't say, but what I suspected was on his mind, was that it wasn't just a question of *when* the others would get back.

It was a question of *if.*

What would happen if the Wentar, Albert, and Ludmilla were caught in Flinduvia?

Maybe that was why he was shaky. After all, this was his family we were talking about.

As IT TURNED OUT, the return of the others was one thing we *didn't* have to worry about. When we got upstairs—all the way upstairs, to Gaspar's lab— we found Albert, Ludmilla, and the Wentar waiting for us.

With them was a skinny, dark-haired boy, not much older than me. He was dressed in a one-piece outfit that looked as if someone had made a pair of coveralls out of blue aluminum foil.

"Martin!" cried Gaspar in astonishment.

"Martin?" echoed Sarah, Gramma, and I all at the same time. (Actually, Grampa said it, too, but I was the only one who could hear him.)

"But he's just a kid!" I said.

"Of course he's still a youngster," said the Wen- tar, who was standing behind the boy, looking gloomy as usual. "He's been in suspended animation for nearly a century!"

Martin was staring up at Gaspar with an expression that seemed half fearful, half hungry. Suddenly I realized how strange it must be for this boy to see his twin as a grown man. It was a good thing Gaspar had at least gotten rid of his lizard head (something Ludmilla and Albert had seemed only moderately surprised to notice).

Martin uttered a few words in a foreign language. That was a surprise, but only because I was being sort of stupid. Of course he spoke a foreign language. The Flinduvians had kidnapped him when he was still a kid living in Transylvania, and they had had him in suspended animation ever since. What did I think he would speak? Basic American?

The second, and much bigger, surprise came when Gaspar answered in the same language, and I realized I could understand it!

I blinked and looked at Sarah. She appeared to be as startled as I was. Then she smiled. "The translation spell!" she exclaimed. "It's still working!"

What Gaspar had said was, "So, the big brother is now the little brother, and the little, the big. Welcome back to the world we know, Martin."

Martin's face quavered. I thought for a moment he was going to cry. But then he got control of himself. It was as if his face froze in place.

I had enough sense of Gaspar by now to realize

that normally he would try to comfort a kid who was feeling as bad as Martin seemed to. But Martin wasn't just any kid. Not only was he Gaspar's twin brother, he was—or had been—the just-barely-older brother. And from what Gaspar had told us, Martin had always taken advantage of that fact. Not only that, during the sixteen years that passed between the time Martin fell into Flinduvia and the time that his replacement clone shrank and froze Gaspar and the others, the family had lived with the belief that the clone was the real Martin.

What a mess! No wonder they all seemed to have feelings that were, to say the least, confused. I tried to imagine what it would be like for me to go to sleep some night, and wake up to find my little sister was now a twenty-six-year-old woman. The idea gave me the willies, and I figured it would have been even weirder if she had been my twin. And weirder still if I had first been rescued from an alien planet and dragged back to a foreign country by someone like the Wentar.

I couldn't blame poor Martin for looking like he wanted to cry!

It was Ludmilla who broke the moment. She went to Martin and put her arms around him. "Poor little brother," she whispered.

This gesture might have been more comforting

to Martin if she had not shown her vampire fangs while she spoke. Looking startled, he pulled away from her. "Leave me alone!" he shouted.

Then he put his face in his hands and began to sob.

Her own lips quivering, Ludmilla dropped her hands to her sides and stepped back. At the same time, Gaspar went to stand beside Martin. He said nothing, only put one hand gently on the boy's shoulder.

Martin pushed away and bolted for the door.

Albert and I both started after him. Before we had taken two steps the Wentar raised his hand and made a weird gesture.

Martin slumped to the floor.

Bob dropped into a crouch and growled at the Wentar.

"What have you done?" cried Melisande.

"It is merely a spell of sleep," said the Wentar quietly. "He will rest in comfort while we talk. And we must talk, for there is a great deal to say, and not much time to say it."

Who's the tall, bossy guy? asked Grampa.

It's a long story, I thought back.

That's all right. I think I can figure it out on my own if I just look around in here a bit.

I blinked and shook my head. *Hey! No fair poking around in my head without my permission!*

It's all right, Anthony. Believe me, once you're dead,

you'll find a lot of stuff you used to take seriously isn't really all that important. For example, I already stumbled across a memory that told me it was you who broke that cellar window three years ago. I would have been mad at the time. Now—eh, there's more important stuff to worry about.

I started to answer him, but the Wentar recaptured our attention by saying, "Martin has already given us some vital information—namely, why the Flinduvians want Earth's dead."

"And just why is that?" asked Gaspar.

"They intend to use them to reanimate dead Flinduvian warriors."

"Well, that's just silly," said Melisande. "If they can do that, why don't they just use the souls of their own dead?"

The Wentar made a sniffing sound. "A more cynical being than I might say it is because Flinduvians have no souls. However, like most simple answers, that is not accurate. The real reason is more complicated."

He glanced over at Martin, as if to make sure he was still asleep, and then continued. "Though the Starry Doors provide a wonderful way to travel from world to world, that very ease of transport carries with it the possibility of evil."

"Why?" asked Sarah.

"Because if it were unlimited, it would allow renegade planets to launch massive invasions of other worlds without warning. Of course, the Coalition doesn't have many planets like that, since we carefully screen worlds before we allow them access to the doors. Even so, errors sometimes happen."

"Like the Flinduvians?" asked Gaspar.

"Precisely," said the Wentar. "Allowing the creatures of the red haze into the Coalition of Civilized Worlds was one of our few mistakes, and one of our worst. They are subdued now, and have been for some time. But their planet is a world where great evil lies sleeping. It would not take much to waken it, for the Flinduvians have a lust for conquest. To guard against such peoples using the doors improperly, those who designed them specified that no more than ten members of a species can pass through a gate on any given day."

"I still don't understand what this has to do with Earth's ghosts," I said.

"I'll be glad to explain," snarled a voice from behind me.

I turned, then screamed.

The Flinduvians had arrived.

18

The Flinduvian Plan

THE FIRST TIME I saw a Flinduvian, it had been tearing its way through the barrier that separated the magical corridor leading out of Morley Manor from our own world. I had gotten only a peek, then, because just as the alien was breaking through we had fled through a Starry Door.

That brief sight had been fairly terrifying. Even so, it had not prepared me for the full horror of the Flinduvians.

To begin with, they were big—between six and eight feet tall. Of course, Gaspar and the Wentar were tall, too. But they didn't have biceps like basket-balls, and thighs as big around as my waist. We're not talking *fat* thighs, either. I could see that they were solid muscle (or whatever Flinduvians have), because the aliens' uniforms consisted of nothing more than tight-fitting shorts, broad silver armbands, and chest harnesses to hold weapons and ammunition. They didn't even wear shoes, which you would think would be a basic item for warrior types. At least, you would think that if you hadn't seen a Flinduvian's foot, which is sort of like a horse's hoof made long and flexible.

Their fingers were even more flexible, because they weren't really fingers but scale-covered tentacles. What really gave me the creeps was that the tentacles were of different lengths and thicknesses. I figured this meant they had specialized uses... something I decided not to think about too much.

The Flinduvians' muscles weren't the only things that bulged. They also had bulging snouts and eyes.

All in all, they were pretty ugly.

Mom has always told us not to judge people by their looks, but I was having a hard time following that advice right then. Not only did the Flinduvians look big, mean, and nasty, my gut was telling me that they probably acted the same way.

There were ten of them, and they pretty much filled the room.

The guy at the front, who I assumed was their leader, smiled.

I wished he hadn't. Not because of the two rows of silvery fangs, though they were bad enough. No, it was the black, snaky tongue flicking out of his mouth that really got to me. It was far more horrible and frightening than Gaspar's had been, probably because it had two big holes in the end of it—holes that opened and closed like sniffing nostrils.

"The plan is simple," he said, in a voice that sounded like pebbles being run through a blender. "While no more than ten members of a species may pass through a gate, that restriction applies only to the living. We can transport as many *corpses* as we wish. Once we have them here, we can inject them with the spirits of Earth's dead, and bring them back to life."

"What good will that do you?" asked Gaspar. "You can't expect Earth's dead to fight on your behalf."

"They'll have no choice," said the Flinduvian cheerfully. "All we need is their life force to animate the body. Once we install them, their actions will be completely under our control."

"And where are you going to get an army's worth of corpses?" asked Gaspar.

The alien smiled again. "No Flinduvian hesitates to die in the service of his planet. When the call goes out for bodies, our biggest problem will be sorting through the many volunteers eager to earn a spot in warrior heaven. Such a death is a great honor, a privilege."

"If you can put a soul into a body, vy don't you just reinsert the one that vas there to begin vith?" asked Ludmilla.

The leader sneered. "Once a body has died, reinstalling a soul can give it power and movement, but not genuine life. These re-animates will be mere zombies." (He didn't actually use the word *zombie,* of course, since he was speaking in Flinduvian. But that was the sense of it.) "To be trapped in such a thing is not a proper fate for the soul of a Flinduvian hero. It would be an insult to his honor. That's why it was such a great boost to our plans when we captured young Martin there. By studying him, we eventually discovered what an absurdly strong connection to life the ghosts of this miserable, long-ignored little planet of yours possess—strong enough to make them cling even to an alien body. It makes them perfect for our uses."

He threw back his head and laughed. At least, I think it was a laugh. The actual sound was sort of a cross between a chainsaw and a werewolf gargling. "Now, at last, Flinduvia will rouse from her slumber! Now we wake—and the galaxy trembles!"

I heard a groan, and turned to see Martin push

himself to a kneeling position. Melisande started toward him.

"Don't move!" snapped the Flinduvian.

Martin looked up at the sound of his voice. "Oh, it's you, Dysrok! It's about time. I was wondering when you were going to get here."

"Martin, what are you talking about?" cried Gaspar.

"Be quiet, you fool," snapped the boy. "Why do you think I let the Wentar bring me back here? Does the word *bait* mean anything to you?"

Melisande started to cry. Gramma put an arm around her shoulder.

That's my Ethel, thought Grampa. *Always worried about others.*

Though he didn't say anything else, I caught a note of terror running beneath his thoughts. He was right to be terrified. The very moment he sent those words to me, one of the Flinduvian's armbands began to beep.

Dysrok smiled, and his tongue flicked out. "Well," he said happily. "It looks as if we have a ghost near us right now. Might as well collect it while we have the chance. Who knows when it might prove useful?"

The Flinduvian behind him, the one with the beeping armband, turned in a slow circle. When he was facing in my direction, the armband began to beep more loudly. His blue face creased in one of those horrible, tongue-flicking smiles, and he stepped toward me.

The beeping increased.

Dysrok looked puzzled. "Are you harboring one of the dead, boy?"

I shook my head, trying to look both innocent and stupid.

It did no good. The Flinduvian with the armband raised his hand. He was holding something shaped like a big squirt gun—colorful and bulgy, with a wide mouth at one end and a yellow, bottlelike thing at the other. He smiled, his snaky tongue flicking out at me. The big black holes in its tip opened and closed like sniffing nostrils. "Come out, come out, wherever you are!" he called mockingly.

Then he pointed the collecting gun at my head, and pulled the trigger.

19

The Collecting Jar

I HEARD A CRACKLE, and felt a buzz of energy, a little like the feeling we got when we went through the Starry Doors.

Hold on, Grampa! I thought. *Hold on!*

Someone screamed. (Later, I realized it had been me.)

Then everything went black.

I felt a horrible wrenching, as if I was being pulled apart at the seams. I thought, at first, that it was because Grampa was being ripped from inside me.

It took me a while to realize that the true situation was even worse. It wasn't Grampa who had been ripped out of my body—it was me! *I* was the one who got sucked into the collecting jar!

At first I just felt as if I had fainted or something. Then, for a little while, it was as if I were in a dream—the kind where you know you're dreaming but can't force yourself to wake up. Finally I began to realize where I was.

I screamed again, which was getting to be sort of a habit. It didn't make any difference, since no one could hear me. I suppose it was because I didn't really have a mouth. I didn't have eyes or ears, either, but somehow I could still hear and see what was going on. Don't ask me how that worked. I suppose I was hearing and seeing the same way that ghosts do—the same way I had when we left our bodies to go to the Land of the Dead. I hadn't thought about it as much then, because I was still in a shape that resembled my own body. But being stuffed inside a bottle made you wonder about that sort of thing.

As I began to get a sense of what was going on, I realized that Grampa was putting on a big show.

"How could you just take him like that?" he cried. He was speaking with my voice, through my mouth, and clutching the sides of my head with my hands.

"What's happening?" cried Gramma. "Anthony, what's going on?"

Grampa turned my body toward her and said, "It was Grampa. He was inside me, and they pulled him out!"

A cold fear gripped me. What was Grampa doing? Was he planning to *keep* my body? Was it possible my own grandfather would betray me that way? But why else would he be lying to her like that?

Gramma was furious. "You let my husband out of that bottle!" she cried, lunging at the Flinduvian who held the collecting gun.

"Ethel!" cried Gaspar. He caught her and held her back.

Dysrok laughed. "We'll let the ghost out when the time is right. Out of the bottle . . . and into the body of a Flinduvian warrior. His life force will animate that body, but control of it will be ours. He will be a perfect slave."

Gramma didn't understand any of that, of course, since she hadn't had a translation spell put on her. But I did, and believe me, it didn't do anything to make me feel better about my situation.

What made things even worse was when the Flinduvian yanked the bottle off the end of his gun and dropped it into a pack he was carrying. Everything went dark. I couldn't see or hear a thing.

I had just come back from the Land of the Dead.

In my opinion, this was far worse.

The only good thing about being stuffed into the pack was that it gave me a chance to think. In fact, thinking was about the only thing I *could* do under the circumstances. Actually, that's not quite true. I could also *panic,* which was the first thing I did. Not that it did me any good. I mean, usually when you panic you run around and scream, or hyperventilate, or something like that. All I could do was feel like I *wanted* to do that stuff. That feeling kept growing and growing, until I thought I was going to explode. That might not have been all bad. Maybe the bottle would have exploded, too, which might have been kind of cool—though I don't know if I would have zapped back into my body, or just been left floating around like a ghost.

A living ghost. What a weird thing to be.

When you panic, you're supposed to take deep breaths. Since I had no nose, mouth, lungs, or air, I couldn't do that. Finally I started to pray. That helped. I didn't get a miracle or anything, but I did settle down—which was sort of a miracle all by itself, if you consider my circumstances.

Once I finally got calmer, I was able to start thinking. The first thing I needed to think about was why Grampa was pretending to be me. I finally decided he was trying to fake out the aliens. Maybe he figured if they thought they had a ghost, but had really gotten the spirit of a *living* person, there might be some advantage to keeping that fact from them.

At least, I hoped that was what he was thinking. Part of me was afraid that what he was really thinking was, "Yippee! I'm alive again!"

The second thing I needed to think about was why the Flinduvian collecting gun had taken me and left Grampa in my body. I came up with two theories that sort of made sense. The first came from Dysrok's statement that Earth's ghosts have an "absurdly strong" connection to life. Maybe Grampa, having already experienced death, was clinging to life more tightly than I did. The second possible reason was our recent trip to the Land of the Dead. Since I had already been out of my body, and not that long ago, maybe I wasn't as tightly connected to it as I should have been.

Or maybe it was the two things put together. I was in uncharted territory here. And ever if one of those theories did explain why I had gotten pulled out of my body, they didn't tell me what I really needed to know—namely, what should I do next?

Of course, when you've been yanked out of your body, stuck inside a bottle, and then crammed into an alien's backpack, your options for action are pretty limited.

So is your sense of time. I had no idea how long I

had been in the bottle panicking, praying, thinking, and fussing before one of the Flinduvians opened the pack and pulled me out again.

Holding up my prison, he said, "Let's give this one a try. Bring in one of the corpses. We'll put him inside and see how it works."

20

I Become
a Flinduvian

THE FLINDUVIANS carried in a box that looked something like a coffin. It was bigger than most coffins—though given how big the Flinduvians were, that made sense. It was also very plain, with no decorations or fancy woodwork or anything. The only marks on it at all were some squiggles across the top, which might have been Flinduvian writing. Suddenly I realized that the squiggles looked like the marks on the box where the Martin-clone had imprisoned Gaspar and the others.

The Flinduvians stood the coffin upright. Dysrok touched a button on its side.

The front swung open.

Inside stood the hulking figure of a dead Flinduvian.

My new home.

Like the other Flinduvians, this guy had muscles on his muscles, tentacles instead of fingers, and feet that looked like long, flexible horse hooves. Even though its eyes were closed, I could tell they were big and bulgy. So was its snout, with its upthrust fangs.

They carried the collecting bottle over and connected it to a pipe on the side of the box.

Then they pumped me inside the Flinduvian.

At first I felt only a horrid clamminess, as if I had been wrapped in a piece of raw liver. Then, slowly, the body began to come back to life. I could feel the alien blood pumping through its alien veins. I would have screamed again, but I couldn't; the body was not mine to control, merely to inhabit.

My eyes blinked open and I could see again.

Seeing the world as a Flinduvian was very different from seeing it as an Earthling. First, colors did not look the same. It wasn't as simple as them looking lighter or darker than usual. They looked like nothing I had ever seen before. It's hard to explain clearly, but I have to tell you, it was pretty freaky.

Second, Flinduvian eyes are much sharper than ours. I could see things I had never seen before: the texture of clothing, the flecks of color in the eyes of someone twenty feet away. I could count the individual hairs on Gaspar's hand.

But along with that sharpness came something that I can only describe as "interpretation." Every object I saw seemed like either a potential danger or a potential weapon—sometimes both at once. And every non-Flinduvian being, even my sweet old grandmother, looked like a menace and an enemy. If it hadn't been for the lucky fact that I had no control over the body I was in, I might have rushed forward to crush her.

I did not like being a Flinduvian. But at least I could see why they were so nasty—though I wondered if they saw things this way because they were so nasty, or they were so nasty because of the way they saw things.

Dysrok took a black box from his pack. He turned a dial, and I felt a jolt of power tingle through me. It was scary, but not totally unpleasant.

"There," he said. "He's been activated. Zarax, step forward."

Must be Zarax was my name, because I had no choice but to step forward.

Dysrok smiled. "See how simple it is? It takes

only moments to reactivate the body with one of your ghosts. Once done, that body is completely under our command."

"What about the ghost itself?" asked Gaspar. "What happens to it?"

Dysrok's tongue flicked out. "The ghost is merely a battery—a life force to energize the body. And since the device that prevents more than ten members of a species from passing through a Starry Door on any given day does not apply to corpses, we can bring through a million of these warriors-in-waiting if need be. With a small advance group in place to activate them, we can transport an army large enough to conquer this puny planet in a matter of hours."

He stretched his chest triumphantly. "Once the planet is ours, the real work begins. We will harvest your ghosts. Then, using them as fuel for our warriors' bodies, we will take our rightful place as rulers of the galaxy."

I thought about the sorrowful spirits we had met in the Land of the Dead, and imagined them being imprisoned in Flinduvian bodies as I now was. I thought about Grampa being stuck here. I thought about old Mr. Zematoski from across the street, who had died last month, and Edon Farrell's big sister, Gwen, who had been killed in a car accident two years ago. The idea of their spirits being stuffed into these cold Flinduvian corpses was so appalling it made me want to twitch.

To my surprise, one of my new arms *did* twitch.

What made this surprising was that I was not supposed to have any control of the Flinduvian body at all.

I tried to do it again.

Nothing.

I focused my thoughts, putting all my energy into moving the right hand.

Nothing ... nothing ... nothing ... *Twitch!*

I stopped immediately. I didn't want the Flinduvians to know what I was up to. I tried to glance around to see if any of them had noticed, but twitch or not, I didn't have control of my eyes. All I could do was look straight ahead at the parlor of Morley Manor, which was fairly crowded, despite the fact that all the furniture was gone.

Gramma and Sarah and all the members of the Family Morleskievich were looking at me. Sarah was crying. I wanted to wave, to signal somehow that I was alive and well, but couldn't manage it. The weirdest thing of all was seeing my own body, from which Grampa was staring at me with horror and fascination.

I had no idea what to do next.

It didn't make any difference; Dysrok decided for

me. Twisting the dial on his control panel, he sent me to stand against the wall.

"Close your eyes and wait for future orders," he said.

I did as I was told.

The darkness was complete. I couldn't move. The Flinduvian body, though animated by my spirit, remained the coldest thing I had ever experienced.

I wanted to shiver, but couldn't. It was, I suppose, a lot like being dead.

No, that's not really true. If I had been dead, I could have moved on to the Land of the Dead, which, strange as it is, would have been better than this living coffin of cold Flinduvian flesh.

Then I realized that this was what they wanted to do to all of Earth's dead, or at least as many as they could harvest.

It made me want to scream.

21

The Haunted Body

MY SIGHT WAS GONE. I had nothing to feel or taste. But I did have two working senses: I could hear, and I could smell. As I began to settle into the body, I realized it was not only Flinduvian eyes that were sharper than ours. My new nose was much sharper as well. It took me longer to get used to that, simply because I wasn't used to smelling things so clearly. And a lot of what I could smell I couldn't figure out, because I didn't know how to interpret it.

Still, by listening carefully and paying attention to

the information coming from my snout, I began to associate specific smells with specific people. (Or aliens, or monsters; whatever.) Once I had figured that out, I began to be able to get a sense of where people were standing, and when they moved. After a while I also realized that their odors *changed* when they were talking. I could actually smell fear, anger, and confidence.

As time went on it became clear that the Flinduvians were waiting for some higher officer who was supposed to take charge of the situation.

"Where is Jivaro?" growled Dysrok, two or three times.

The sound of his heavy footsteps told me he was pacing back and forth across the floor. By tracing his smell, I could tell exactly the route he was taking.

"Who cares?" asked one of the other Flinduvians. "Why don't we just destroy these fools and get it over with?"

Dysrok walked over to him. Though the soldier made no cry of pain or protest, from the sound of things I got the impression that he was getting smacked upside the head a couple of times.

"Because, you moron," roared Dysrok, when he was done whacking the other guy, "the only one really worth killing is the Wentar, and we can't do *that* without a higher officer present."

"You'd be wiser not to do it at all," said the Wentar in peaceful tones.

"Hold your tongue, arrogant nitwit!" snarled Dysrok. The anger in his voice was terrifying. Yet he didn't take a step toward the Wentar, or any of the others. Given how much trouble the Wentar had gotten us into, I was glad to know that he was of some use.

"Oy," said Albert. "Maybe we should have stayed in the box."

"Silence!" thundered Dysrok.

While all this was going on, I continued struggling with the body I was in, trying to get control of it. It was hard to tell if I was succeeding, since I didn't dare make any big movements. I couldn't even try opening my eyes, since that would alert them to what I was doing.

Mostly I tried clenching my butt muscles.

That may sound stupid, but can you think of anything else you can move when it's a matter of life and death that no one in front of you notice the slightest twitch?

I was also sort of exploring the body, trying to get used to it—to its size and its power, its weird differences from a human body. Some of those differences were obvious—the tentacles I now possessed in place of regular fingers, the weird, hooflike feet. Some were less obvious—like the incredible strength. (The reason that was less obvious was because I had no way of using it.)

As time went on I began to settle more deeply into the body. I figured this was good, because it would make it more likely I could get control of it at some point. But it also made me nervous. What if by settling in I got so connected to the body that I could never get out again?

That was a terrifying thought. It got even more terrifying when I began to find bits and pieces of the previous owner's memories clinging to the brain.

Who knows how the connection of mind and body, spirit and flesh, really works? Not me, so don't ask me to explain this. But it was pretty eerie, let me tell you; as if I wasn't in the body alone. Well, not quite; the previous owner was clearly gone. Yet his memories lingered on, like the furniture, photos, and knickknacks left behind in an old house after its owner has died.

This adventure had started in a haunted house. Now I found myself in a haunted body. And certainly the first of its memories that I experienced scared me as much as a cold hand grabbing you in a dark room—partly because it seemed to come out of nowhere. I would have jumped in terror, except I couldn't, of course, since I had no control of the body. Even so, I did feel it flinch a bit.

The memory was as intense as my best daydreams, and deeply terrifying. The terror came because my immediate reaction was that the alien who had originally owned the body was still in it after all—that I was trapped in this body with its own ghost.

"Get me out of here!" I wanted to cry.

If I had been in a room instead of a body, I would have beat at the door with my fists, flung myself against it, trying to break it down.

But this body had no door.

The memory itself was simple enough: It was of standing on a mountaintop, staring at a city far below. Even though the city was squat and ugly, the view had a kind of stark beauty. The sky—high, wide, and light green—was lit by two suns. The city sat beside a dark lake. Beyond it stretched a scorched desert, open and arid, but vivid red against the pale green sky.

Yet there was no pleasure connected to the memory, only a flash of terrible fear and loneliness. More information bubbled up, and I suddenly understood that the memory was from a childhood day when my body's owner had been abandoned on that mountaintop in order to toughen him up.

Clearly, growing up Flinduvian was not easy.

Other memories began to surface, like bubbles rising in a glass of soda: memories of fear, of being hit, of being trained to be cruel and ferocious. The one that still haunts me most is of being locked in a room with three other kids, and only enough water for two of us to stay alive until the day we were scheduled to be released.

I can't talk about that one in any more detail. It still upsets me too much.

I almost began to feel sorry for these guys—though that sure didn't mean I wanted to let them take over the Earth, much less the entire galaxy.

The problem was, how could we stop them?

I certainly didn't expect an answer to my question. I got one, anyway. It sounded unexpectedly in my head, seeming to come from nowhere: *All we have to do is let the Coalition of Civilized Worlds know what they're up to.*

This sudden communication was even scarier than the alien memories, and I think I actually managed to flinch. That was pretty minor, considering that what I wanted to do was grab the sides of my head and scream "Who are you? What are you doing in here?"

I couldn't, of course. But I guess I managed to think it, since the voice answered me.

This is Martin.

22

Martin's Story

MARTIN? I thought in astonishment. *As in Gaspar's brother? As in the kid that the Flinduvians brought back with them?*

No, Martin the next-door neighbor's dog. Of course I'm Gaspar's brother.

But how did you get in here—into this body?

The Flinduvians have put me in and pulled me out of more bodies than I can count. After a while I learned to do it on my own—though I never let them know I could do it. Now, are you going to waste my time with stupid questions, or shall we try to figure out a way to solve this mess?

You got any suggestions? I thought, hoping that didn't qualify as a stupid question.

Martin sighed. *Unfortunately, no. But now that I've managed to get in contact with you, at least we'll be in better shape if an opportunity does arise.*

That was fine with me. It was the first glimmer of hope I'd had since the Flinduvians showed up. But I was still curious. So despite the crack about stupid questions, I tried another. *I don't get it. Whose side are you on—ours, or the Flinduvians'?*

My own, he replied sharply.

Care to explain that? I asked.

Depends on how much time we have, he answered. *Let me go check.*

I didn't feel him go, but I guess he must have, because suddenly he said, *All right, it looks like everything is quiet out there.*

Don't they notice when you leave your body? I asked.

Actually, it's possible they could, and that's a danger. But I've just been sitting in the corner looking sullen and no one is paying much attention to me. Even if they do glance my way, it just appears that I'm resting my head on my arms. Now, let me fill you in on some of the details of what's happening.

Here's his story. A couple of points I figured out later, but for the most part, this is what he said:

———

WHEN I FIRST FELL through the worlds into Flinduvia, I was nearly as pleased as I was terrified. At last, it seemed, my quest for greater knowledge of the worlds beyond ours was to be rewarded. Little did I know that the reward would carry with it its own punishment. But that was the case, for in stumbling into Flinduvia, I had entered a place that was as close to a living hell as you will ever find.

Given what I had learned about Flinduvia from being trapped in the alien body, I had no trouble believing this.

When I tumbled out of our world, there was a Flinduvian waiting to snatch me up. They had detected the reckless experiments Gaspar and I were conducting, and had created a kind of trap, hoping we would stumble into it.

It took very little time for them to make a copy of me and send it back to Earth. Not a clone; the clones came later. This was a quick copy job, little more than an animated puppet to hold my place. Within a few days it was replaced by a more sophisticated copy, and a few weeks later another. Finally they had a perfect clone of me, which they programmed as they wished, then sent off as my final replacement. It studied both my family and our world, sending back information to its masters. But because they had a need to make it believable, the clone had a combination of human and Flinduvian characteristics, which is one reason that it shared some of the great secrets with my family, such as the Starry Doors. The Flinduvians were unhappy about *that—partly because if it had been discovered that they had let the secret out to a planet not part of the Coalition of Civilized Worlds the punishment would have been swift and severe. But they felt the risk was worth the possible gain.*

Meanwhile, I was being held prisoner. Or perhaps it would be more accurate to say I was kept as an experimental lab animal. I was poked, prodded, and analyzed as completely and impersonally as if I were some important new species of insect.

Yet after a time, some of them began to talk to me, to tell me about things. I got the feeling they looked on me as we might look on a particularly intelligent pet: someone to share your troubles with. Certainly a Flinduvian would never share his troubles or doubts with another of his own species. That would be seen as weakness, which is the most dangerous trait you can display in their society.

Now, time in Flinduvia flows differently than it does here, at a ratio of about three to one. That's one reason they were able to send back that first copy in what seemed such a short time to Gaspar: for every minute that passes here, three minutes go by on Flinduvia.

Which means that I, myself, have been there for the equivalent of over two hundred years.

There was such weariness and sorrow in that statement that it nearly broke my heart. But it also confused me. *If you've been there so long, how come you still look like you're only twelve?*

Because this was the body the Flinduvians thought

would work best as bait when the Wentar and the others showed up. Besides, even though I have been several different ages, physically speaking, during my time on Flinduvia they liked keeping me as they had first captured me. I think I was a symbol of their first step toward the conquest they dreamed of.

Anyway, as the years rolled on, as the first century moved into the second, I earned more and more privileges from the scientists who guarded and studied me. One of those was the ability to occasionally don other versions of my body. I could be myself as I would appear at twenty, or thirty, or forty, and so on. They kept dozens of copies of me in their lab, and with their technology it was not that hard to move from one to another.

Which is how I was able to come back to Earth when I discovered that they had called home the clone that had been taking my place here. They knew I hated being in the old man versions of my body, so they didn't put many safeguards on them. Late one night, I slipped into one of those bodies, then through the Starry Door that leads to this house. I was horrified to discover that the contents were being sold. I had only a little time before I would be missed in Flinduvia. I didn't want to take my family back there, but I had to make sure they were taken out of the house before the place was destroyed. That was why I showed your sister the box where my clone had placed my frozen, shrunken family so long ago.

How did you know about that? I asked him.

The Flinduvians told me, the fools. Because they have no family bonds at all, and because they knew I had had many conflicts with my brother and sisters, my captors simply assumed that what they had done to my family wouldn't make that much difference to me. They actually thought it might amuse me.

His voice grew scornful. *Vile Flinduvians! They did not understand the ties that bind the Family Morleskievich! Blinded by their own cruelty, they could never guess the bonds of blood and loyalty I share with my brother and sisters, no matter how much I might have fought with them. Nor could they ever begin to realize how deeply I desired to free my family, how I would plot for decade after decade to release them.*

He was silent for a moment, and I got a sense he was brooding about his centuries on Flinduvia. I tried to put myself in his place, imagine what it was like. The idea gave me cold shivers.

Finally he spoke again:

Now, here's what you need to know, Anthony. The key to the entire Flinduvian plan is secrecy. If word of what they're up to gets back to the High Council of the Coalition of Civilized Worlds, the Coalition's massed forces will clamp down on the Flinduvians faster than a mousetrap snapping shut. The Council is suspicious, but this is High Diplomacy, and there are delicate rules to be followed. To have any chance of success, the Flinduvians must have their conquest well under way before anyone realizes what is going on.

So all we really need to do is break up this situation long enough for the Wentar to get back to his home world and pass on this information. It would be nice if we got out of this alive, but given what's at stake, living through it is really a side issue.

Are you telling me that the fate of the civilized galaxy rests in our hands? I asked.

I'd say that's an accurate statement of the situation, Martin replied. *But then— Wait! Let's listen.*

An argument had broken out among the Flinduvians. Actually, their regular conversations could be considered arguments, so this was something bigger.

"We should not wait for Jivaro!" shouted one of the warriors, one who had not spoken before. "Let's kill them now and be done with it."

"Who is in command here, Frax?" shouted Dysrok.

"The question is, who *should* be in command?" replied Frax, giving Dysrok a shove.

Martin must have sensed my astonishment that a soldier would shove his leader, because he said, *They're like this all the time. A position of power is yours for no longer than you can hold it. They shift— Uh-oh!*

Frax, getting louder and angrier, had shoved his way past Dysrok. "We'll start with the old lady," he said. "Just for fun."

I could smell him moving toward my grandmother. In vain, I ordered my body to act, struggling desperately to lift an arm, take a step. No luck. I stood as if frozen.

My little sister had no such problem. "You leave my gramma alone!" Sarah screamed. I could smell her fear—and her anger, which was at least as strong. I smelled her leaping over to stand in front of Gramma.

"You'll do just as well for starters!" roared Frax, snatching her off the floor.

Sarah's scream filled the room.

23

The Red Haze

THAT WAS IT. Sarah might be a total pain-in-the-butt sister, but she was *my* pain in the butt, and I didn't intend to let any stinking alien turn her into sister sushi.

"Let her go, you damn Flinduvian!" I screamed.

At the same time my eyes snapped open. A haze of red colored my vision, and I could feel myself taking control of the body at last.

Bellowing with rage, I charged forward.

"Zarax, stop!" commanded Dysrok.

I laughed. As if I was going to stop simply because he told me to! I was a creature of fierce power and furious anger. The red haze had me, and no mere order would stop my onslaught!

Dysrok fiddled with the control box, twisting the knob, shaking the box, shaking it harder, finally flinging it to the floor so fiercely that it burst into pieces.

I reached out with my fist and smashed him in the face as I went past. He fell with a thud.

The red haze grew brighter.

The alien who had picked up Sarah looked at me in fear and astonishment.

"You . . . put . . . her . . . *down!*" I roared, the words coming out in the harsh language of Flinduvia.

Somewhere in my head I could hear Martin laughing.

The Flinduvian dropped Sarah. Immediately Ludmilla and Melisande swooped in and snatched her away from the battle.

And a battle it was. The Flinduvian I had challenged had started to pummel me. I didn't care. My blood was like fire. I was in a frenzy, a creature of the red haze, a roaring, shrieking, fighting machine.

Two other aliens jumped me from behind. I tried to shake them off, but they clamped on to me and dragged me to the floor.

Then, suddenly, complete chaos erupted in the

room. It took me a moment to realize what had happened. Gaspar, sensing the moment was right, did what he had not had a chance to do before. Digging into his pocket, he pulled out the sonic disruptor that the Wentar had given him back on the Planet of the Frogs. He flung the silvery disk to the floor.

It exploded in a cloud of smoke that gave off bright flashes of color. As each flash burst, it emitted a high squeal that seemed to go right through my head. It must have been pitched to some note that was particularly excruciating to the Flinduvians, because all of them (me, included) slammed their hands to their ears and began to howl.

The humans in the room looked at us in astonishment, as if they couldn't figure out what we were doing.

The pain was incredible, so intense and debilitating that I suspect it came from more than just the sound. But Flinduvian warriors are trained to ignore pain. So the sonic disruptor proved to be no more than what the Wentar had said it would be: a distraction.

The other aliens were the first to move against it. Staggering, groaning, they began to lurch toward the device—with the intention of breaking it, I suppose.

I wasn't used to dealing with such pain. I wasn't used to maneuvering this body. But I had one thing in my favor: The Flinduvians were mere soldiers. I was a brother, a grandson, a friend. They were fighting because it was what they did. I was fighting because I had to save people I loved.

I had one more thing in my favor: Martin. He was inside my head, cheering me on.

This isn't your body, Anthony! he cried. *Who cares what happens to it? The pain will end. All that matters is who wins the fight.*

With a roar I threw myself forward, heading for the device myself. The pain was phenomenal, pulsing through my Flinduvian skull like razors of fire coated in acid. But the red haze was stronger. I pushed through the wall of agony, screaming and howling in a voice that scared even me. It was like trying to force yourself upstream through a river of burning molasses. I could see the other Flinduvians, each moving slowly toward the disruptor, ready to smash it, if it was the last thing they ever did.

I had to get there first, to keep the advantage.

I pushed ahead, pushed faster.

"Zarax, I command you to stop!" screamed Dysrok. He was crawling across the floor from the other direction.

Frax, the soldier who had been arguing with him, stepped on his head—a gesture of contempt for his failure, I guess.

One of the Flinduvians grabbed my arm. I spun

and slammed him so viciously it sent him sprawling across the room. Astonished at my own strength, I forged onward. I was about to snatch the disruptor from the floor, turn it toward the others, drive them out of the room, when two Flinduvians tackled me. I hit the floor with a crash that shook the walls.

All the Flinduvians were roaring and screaming.

The smell of their rage, their fear, their hate burned in my alien nostrils, filling the *real* me with horror. Yet at the same time, it seemed to give added power to the alien body.

The red haze still clouded my vision. With a roar, I picked up one of the Flinduvians who had tackled me and smashed him against the other. Both fell unconscious.

I started crawling toward the disruptor again. The closer I got, the more I felt as if my head was going to explode.

So what if it explodes? Martin screamed through the blazing pain. *It's not your head! Keep going! KEEP GOING!*

I had almost reached the device when one of the Flinduvians grabbed my feet. I tried to pull myself forward, but it was hard to move *toward* so much pain, hard when the enemy was trying to pull me away from it and each inch I slid backward offered a shred of blessed relief.

Suddenly I heard a vicious snarling and snapping.

Bob, sweet little cocker spaniel Bob, had attacked the Flinduvian holding my foot. The alien shouted in anger. He didn't let go, but the attack distracted him enough for me to shake myself free.

I pulled myself another few inches closer to the Wentar's silvery disk.

Now I realized that the others had thrown themselves into the battle. Albert was leaping around the room, bounding against the staggering aliens, trying to keep them from reaching me. I saw him scramble onto a table, launch himself into the air, then land on a Flinduvian's back.

"Yahoo!" he cried, covering its bulging eyes with his hands. "Just like the old days, huh, boss?"

Gaspar didn't answer; he was too busy pounding on the head of one of the aliens. He was perched on its back and had his legs wrapped around its waist. "Vile disruptor of families!" he snarled, giving the Flinduvian another jolting blow. "Now does the Family Morleskievich take its revenge!"

Not far past him Melisande and Ludmilla were holding another Flinduvian by the legs. Every time the alien reached for one of the sisters, the other one would distract him. Gramma was hitting him on the head with her shoe.

But the strangest sight of all in that mad melee was that of my own human body, powered by

Grampa. Side by side with Sarah, it was pushing one of the monsters away from the disk—away from me.

No human could stand against a Flinduvian in its full strength, of course. But the Wentar's sonic disruptor with its agonizing sounds keyed to Flinduvian ears had weakened our enemies enough for my friends and family to hold them back.

Even so, they were risking their lives to do it.

I couldn't let them down.

With a last surge of strength I lunged forward and grabbed the sonic disruptor. I staggered to my feet. The Flinduvians howled in rage. Feeling as if a thousand bombs were exploding in my brain, I pointed the device at them, and began to herd them toward one side of the room.

Well done! cried Martin. *Well done, Anthony!*

"Watch out!" cried Grampa, from my body's mouth.

I turned, just in time to see one of the Flinduvians lunging toward me. I kicked savagely, catching him in the jaw and sending him reeling back against the wall.

"Enough," said the Wentar, stepping forward. "Enough. It is finished."

Gently, he took the sonic disruptor from my hands.

Pain overwhelmed me.

I collapsed to the floor, and into a well of blackness.

24

Martin's Choice

WHEN I OPENED my eyes, my friends and family were staring down at me.

I did a quick check. If I had had a heart, it would have sunk.

I was still in the Flinduvian body.

"Horace, are you all right in there?" asked Gramma.

"That's not Horace, darling," said my grandfather, who was standing next to her, still wrapped in my body. "It's Anthony."

"If that's Anthony, then who are *you*?" cried Sarah, looking at my body nervously.

"I'm your grandfather," he said, sounding slightly embarrassed.

Sarah's eyes got wide. "This is *too* weird," she said, backing away from him.

"I don't understand," said Gramma, her voice quavering. She looked as if she was about to cry. "I don't understand any of this!"

"I'm sorry, Ethel," said Grampa gently. "When those monsters snatched Anthony out of his body instead of me, it seemed best not to say anything. I figured anything they didn't know might be helpful to us later on."

"A wise choice," said the Wentar. "Information is always a useful tool. I suspect the reason Anthony was able to seize control of the Flinduvian body was that he is a living spirit, not a dead one. Your silence may well have provided the element of surprise we needed to overcome them."

"So you weren't planning to keep my body?" I asked.

"Of course not!" said Grampa. He sounded indignant, but my face had just enough of a blush on it that I suspected the idea had crossed his mind. Oh well. If the situation was reversed, I probably would have considered it, too. It's what you do that counts, not what you think about doing, thank goodness.

"So how do we get me out of this thing?" I asked, looking down at my horrible alien body.

"I'm not sure," said the Wentar, sounding uncomfortable.

"Could you use that Flinduvian collecting gun?" asked Sarah. "If it put him in there, shouldn't it be able to pull him out?"

"It's worth a try," said the Wentar, his long face looking gloomy.

"What happened to the Flinduvians, anyway?" I asked. My head was still throbbing, and it was hard for me to concentrate.

"The Ventar called for assistance vile you vere sleeping," said Ludmilla, sounding very satisfied. "The group that vas here vas hauled avay. I hope they vill receive terrible justice."

"Once I had proof of their plans, it was easy to get the Coalition of Civilized Worlds to slap a quarantine on their planet," said the Wentar. "I had long suspected that they were plotting something, but it was impossible to act without evidence. They will not be a menace again for a very long time."

"Here's the gun," said Albert, clumping back over to join us. "Who wants to try?"

"I will," said Martin. "I know their technology best."

He pointed the collecting gun at my head. I flinched. On the other hand I couldn't wait to get out of that horrible body.

"Ready?" asked Martin.

I nodded.

He pulled the trigger. A surge of energy surrounded me. Everything went black.

WHEN I OPENED my eyes, I was still trapped inside the Flinduvian.

"What happened?" I cried in horror.

"Nothing," whispered Melisande, lowering her head in sorrow. "Nothing at all."

"I believe I know the source of the problem," said the Wentar.

"What?" I cried. "What is it?"

"When you went into the red haze, you meshed yourself with the Flinduvian body in a deep way. You were not merely inhabiting it, not merely providing it with energy. You were *living* in it, in the way it was accustomed to. Now it doesn't want to let go of you."

"Does that mean I have to spend the rest of my life as a Flinduvian?" I asked in horror.

No one answered. No one looked happy.

"Maybe I could take his place?" suggested Grampa.

Gramma gasped, but didn't say anything.

"It might work," said the Wentar. "But it would be a bad idea. If I'm correct, and the reason Anthony could seize control of the body is that his spirit was still a living one, you would have no such advantage. It is more likely you would end up a mindless slave, as the Flinduvians had intended."

"Oh, that's all right," said Grampa. "I was married for nearly fifty years."

"Horace!" cried Gramma in a shocked voice.

"Just joking," he said softly, and I could tell that the point of the joke had been to hold back his own horror at what he might have to do to free me. I felt guilty for having doubted him before.

"I think I have a better idea," said Martin. "*I* will take over the body. I am already used to switching bodies, since the Flinduvians moved me from clone to clone more times than I can count."

The others started to question him, but he raised his hands. Turning to the Wentar, he said, "It would be a good idea, would it not, to have a spy among the Flinduvians—someone who could pass undetected? In case they decide to . . . act up again?"

"I suspect it would," said the Wentar uneasily.

"Then it might as well be me."

Melisande started to cry. Martin actually smiled. "Don't be sad, sister dearest," he said gently. "I have been too long gone from this world to ever fit here comfortably again. Horrible as Flinduvia is, I belong there now. As I told you while Anthony was sleeping, it's been well over two centuries by their time— nearly twenty times as long as I lived on this world.

Besides," he said, smiling wickedly, "I have some scores to settle there."

And so it was decided.

It wasn't easy. Before we even started, Gaspar and Martin went apart from the rest of us. They sat and talked for a long time. I wondered what it was like for them, to have been twins, to have lost each other, for Gaspar to have lived with a clone of Martin, for Martin to have lived through more than two centuries in that other world. What could they say to each other now?

I tried not to be impatient while they talked, but I ached to be free of the Flinduvian body, and feared that if we waited too long it might not be possible.

At last they came back, looking sad but settled. Gaspar, so much bigger and older and yet in truth so much younger than his twin, had his hand on Martin's shoulder.

They nodded at each other. Then Martin's body slumped, and I felt him come back into the Flinduvian body. Slowly, bit by bit, he replaced my spirit with his. It took hours—the longest, most painful and horrifying hours I had ever known. When he was finally done, we said in one voice, "All right, try the gun again."

The Wentar pointed it at our head and pulled the trigger. Once more the energy engulfed me. But this time it was different. I could feel myself being wrenched from the body, pulled back into the collecting jar. My panic was brief. It was a matter of but moments to put me back in my own body.

Welcome home, Anthony, said my grandfather. His voice was kind, gentle, and just a little bit sad. *You did a good job, kiddo.*

We talked for a little while, probably the most private conversation anyone has ever had. Then he disappeared from my body.

I saw his shape floating before me, looking the way it had in the Land of the Dead.

He drifted over to my grandmother. Stroking her cheek—though not really, of course, since touch is only for the living—he whispered, "I love you so, my darling. Be happy. When the time is right, I'll see you on the other side."

He blew a kiss to Sarah, then made a salute to the others. Turning back to me, he mouthed the word, "Remember."

Then he gave me a wink and faded out of sight.

Epilogue

IT'S BEEN A YEAR now since Sarah and I met the monsters of Morley Manor, and a lot of things have changed.

Morley Manor is one of them. Gaspar managed to prove that he was the rightful heir, and once the legal battle was finished (it took until late spring), he and Albert began work on restoring the mansion to its former glory.

Ludmilla and Melisande spend most of their time in Zentarazna these days, but they are often guests at the old house. Sometimes when they come to visit, Gaspar will have a dinner party, to which he invites Sarah, Gramma Walker, and me. Every once in a while the sisters will have some strange new look. The first time they actually had to tell us who they were, which they seemed to find hilarious. But usually they're in their familiar bodies, Melisande with her snaky hair, Ludmilla with her vampire fangs.

Mom and Dad don't quite understand our connection to Morley Manor. That's all right. As I tell them almost every day, "The world is too vast and strange for any of us to understand all of it."

"You've changed this past year, Anthony," Mom says sometimes. "You're growing up."

Maybe. She seems to say that mostly when I'm helping out at the flower shop. But I've got a reason for that. It was something Grampa said to me during that last conversation, what he told me to remember. It didn't sink in completely at the time; there was too much going on, and I was still pretty rattled. But it keeps coming back to me. I suspect he etched it in my brain somehow, leaving it as a little present for me, because I can still hear him say it, as if he was inside my head even now, instead of—

Well, instead of where he is.

Anthony, all your life people are going to tell you to stop and smell the roses. But they won't usually tell you why. So let me give you one good reason, the one I learned too late. There are no gardens in the Land of the Dead. You have to embrace life now, Anthony—now, while you're still part of it. Grab it to you. See it, feel it, hold it, love it. Don't let it pass you by, boy. Don't shut yourself off from it. Because the truth is, you never know what moment is going to be your last, what scent, what sound, what smell will be the last one you experience. Make it good. Make it real.

Probably pretty good advice, coming from a dead man.

So I spend more time at the flower shop than I used to. I like helping Mom and Dad.

Besides, you never know which rose will be your last.

I also spend a lot of time at Morley Manor, working with Gaspar in his strange laboratory, with its mad mix of magic and science, trying, as he says, to plumb the mysteries of the universe.

I don't suppose we'll ever manage to know it all.

On the other hand, I know a few more things than I used to.

Like what it means to have a family that loves you.

We should all be so lucky.

Bruce Coville's high-school colors were orange and black, his favorite holiday is Halloween, and his grandfather ran a cemetery, so it's no surprise that he loves monsters, aliens, werewolves, curses, ghosts, and vampires. He is the author of more than eighty beloved (and wacky) books including *Armageddon Summer* (written with Jane Yolen), the international bestseller *My Teacher Is an Alien*, and all four novels in the Magic Shop series. A great lover of theater, he regularly joins the Syracuse Symphony Orchestra to perform his stories for audiences, and he also runs a company called Full Cast Audio that creates one-of-a-kind recordings of children's books for listeners of all ages. He lives with his family in Syracuse, New York. You can learn more about him at www.brucecoville.com.